SCOTT

Owatonna U Hockey, 2

RJ SCOTT

V.L. LOCEY

Love Lane Books

Scott, Owatonna U Hockey, 2

Copyright © 2019 RJ Scott, Copyright © 2019 V.L. Locey

Cover design by Meredith Russell, Edited by Sue Laybourn

Published by Love Lane Books Limited

ISBN: 9781785645518

All Rights Reserved

SCOTT

OWATONNA U HOCKEY#2

RJ SCOTT &
V.L. LOCEY

Love Lane Books

ONE

Scott

THE NO-LOOK PASS FROM JOHN WAS SWEET. RIGHT TO MY stick, just as we'd practiced, and for a single shining second I was the best goddamned hockey player in the world. I collected the puck, iced to a stop, reversed my skating, the chilled air whipping my face, and I beat one of their defensemen as if he was standing still. I could envision the puck in the net. Hell, I could taste the goal.

I stickhandled past the other D-man, weaving around him, kicking the puck with my blade, back to my stick. The goalie going low, I deked to my left, saw the netminder wobble as he pushed to stop the puck, and slapped it right at him, aiming for the space above the glove hand. I watched it fly in slow motion, but as soon as it left my stick, I knew I'd let it go a millisecond too soon. The rubber met the posts, the crack of sound an exclamation point to my failure to score.

John was there, collecting the puck, trying to corral it as it jumped and slid around the net, but the defense was too good, and in an instant they were shuttling it between them, heading back up the ice. I slammed a hand against the plexiglass, pushed off, and used the momentum to get myself around the back of the net. Muscles screaming, I followed the puck and the other team, reaching Benoit just as he went low, the puck going high, and that was it, the biscuit was in the net, and we were five goals down.

In the first freaking period.

I hadn't even managed to scrape back a goal that would count. Despondently, we headed back for the change, John's stick tapping my calf.

"Nice one, Scotty," he said as he passed and sat back on the bench.

Nice one? I'd fucking missed. A second later, a softer release, a single skate step, and that would have been a goal. Then we could have taken home at least a score in this sorry excuse for a game. John had to be riding me on this.

"Fuck you, John," I snapped, but I wouldn't look at my fellow skater, because he was such a waste of space right now.

This shitty game was all Ryker's fault.

Ryker was home with his dad and Ten, but why the hell would he need to be with Ten for so long? The Eagles were a hot mess without him, and when we lose today, it will be all on him.

We'd opened up the team to the hotshot asshole, and now for some reason, I was being left out to hang because the rest of them relied so heavily on Mr. Draftee. Coach placed a hand squarely on my shoulder, squeezed it. I got the message.

At least you tried, Scott.

I just wished the rest of the team would try as hard. Acid temper coiled inside me and it hurt.

"What the fuck was that?" I snapped at John.

He turned to me. "What the hell?"

"Where were you? Why didn't you pass earlier?"

He looked at me steadily, his bright blue eyes narrowing. "What's your problem, Scotty?"

"Stop calling me fucking Scotty, and do your fucking job."

He was talking at me, shouting something, but I didn't listen because it wasn't worth it. I wanted back on the ice. I was going to pulverize their D, and I was going to score the next goal if it killed me. Testosterone flooded me, my vision clear, my chest tight with tension.

I'll show them all.

I glanced up to where Dad was sitting, and he was staring back at me, his gaze fixed and stony, disappointment in every line of him.

Oh yeah, I got his message as well.

Shame it was you and not your brother on the ice. He 'd have made that shot easily.

You need to practice, Scott. Stay behind.

Fight for this, Scott. Don't let me the fuck down.

Man up, you loser.

I was out at the next change, muscles loose, breathing harsh, and my focus fixed. We could pull this back. John won the face-off, and I caught the slick pass, avoiding their big D. I was on fire. I was purpose and vengeance all wrapped into one.

The tablets were worth it. They were making me fly. I could do anything. I passed to John, who moved to Brandon, and then it was back to me, tic-tac-toe, I had the disc on my stick, the net was wide open, and I was ready. I wound up to shoot, dismissing the crippling pain in my shoulder, forgetting my dad, the coach, the team. The D-man came from nowhere, hip-checking me, nearly taking me off my skates, and I lost the puck. The whistle sounded, but temper held me in its fiery grip. I threw my stick at the D-man as he skated away. It missed him, and someone gripped me from behind. I rounded on the man, swung my gloved fist, and connected with someone's head, the red mist consuming me, the fire burning so bright I couldn't even see. More arms held me, and there was shouting and screaming. Ben was there. What was my best friend doing up on this end of the ice? He was our goalie. He should've been up in our net. He was in my face talking to me, trying to get me to stop straining for freedom to hit someone else. He took off his mask. I could see his dark eyes, and I know he was talking about something.

"Get back in the net!" I was freaking out. The yelling got louder, the air hot with my temper. Was that me shouting?

A fist connected with my face, and I welcomed the pain because pain actually meant I was alive.

"I want to play!" I yelled trying to get free of the hold, and I lashed out at the people nearest to me, connecting with flesh, feeling like a god.

"Stop him!"

"It's Ben!" John shouted at me. "He's hurt. You laid him out!" The voice permeated the temper and passion, and I tore myself away, my fists up, ready to fight anyone who wanted to touch me.

And then Ben was there, standing in front of me, his

face covered in blood, streams of it running from a gash in his forehead, a terrible flood of scarlet on his dark skin.

"Scott!" he shouted at me, swiping at the blood. "It's me!" He gripped my upper arms, and I shook him off, but he wouldn't let me go that easily, stared right at me, blinking at the blood as it slid around his socket. "Scott, please?"

My head was spinning, the red mist retreating, the effect of the pills that made me fast and strong, slipping away and leaving me a ragged, panting mess.

What had I done? I reached for Ben to touch the wound, and he flinched and skated back.

My best friend was scared of me?

"Off," the referee snapped, then took my arm. I was too exhausted to argue, too overwhelmed to care. I glanced up at Dad, and he was on his feet, looking so goddamn happy to see his son fight.

At least he was proud of me, but at what cost? *What have I done?*

All I felt was sick, and the rest of the game was a blur. The coach held me on the bench. I didn't play again, but he wouldn't let me go to the locker rooms, his face a mask of pity and shock. I was lost, becoming something smaller as I sat miserably, staring at the floor, the adrenaline leaving me shaking and confused.

They said the tablets would make me fly, but no one had said I would crash so hard.

We lost. I don't know by how much, because I didn't care. We headed back to the locker room, everyone deadly quiet, and all I wanted to do was apologize to Ben, who hadn't come back after I'd hit him. He'd need stitches; I'd caught him just above his eyebrow, right where it would cut the worst and bleed like a bitch.

"Okay, Scott, let's do this."

Coach was talking to me, our assistant coach Eddie standing next to him, the two of them staring at me steadily.

"What?" I blinked at the room around me. It was just me and the two coaches. "Where's the rest of the team?"

Coach exchanged a pointed look with Eddie. "We want you to open your locker, Scott."

My locker? What?

"I don't understand."

Coach placed a hand on my shoulder. "It will be okay, Scott. I promise we'll work through this."

Why did I want to cry? Men don't cry. That's what everyone had told me when Luke died and I was all cried out. I leaned into Coach, wanting more, needing a hug. Even as messed up as I was, I didn't miss the irony of the coach being the only one to give me true affection.

Eddie cleared his throat. "You have the right to have someone with you, Scott. We need your permission to see inside your locker, but you shouldn't be here alone."

Who would I ask? My dad? Ben, whom I'd just hurt? Ryker wasn't here.

I didn't want any of them to see anyway. The guy who sold me the pills told me what to do if I was found out, but he'd also warned me to keep my cool even if they made me feel like shit.

I reached for the padlock, entering the familiar numbers, and instead of standing aside and letting Coach see what I had in there, I reached in and pulled out the small tub of tablets, handing it directly to him. I'd memorized what I needed to say, the wording perfect, the description of what I'd taken clear and concise. Anything to mitigate the punishment if they found the pills before I told Coach about them.

"I'm self-reporting that I have been using Androstenedione for exactly five weeks."

Eddie's shoulders fell, and Coach turned the pills over in his hand.

"You need to come with me," he said and took my arm, leading me out of the locker room and into his office. Eddie didn't follow and threw me a look of what I had to think was pity. "Sit down, Scott."

I looked at my feet. I wasn't wearing skates. Where had they gone? I was just in socks, still in uniform, hot and sweaty, and completely out of it. Like the weed I'd tried when I was eleven, a stolen puff from Luke, which had made me see prisms and feel as though nothing could hurt me. That was how I felt now, numb, floating, and a band of pain viciously crushed my skull.

"I won't let this slide," Coach said. "You need help, Scott."

He kept talking, about how I was grieving over Luke, how the pressure of hockey and academia was too much for some people, how I needed so much help I was going to be an old man and still getting therapy. Or at least, it sounded that way.

"… one year suspension, Scott. You understand that, right?"

I nodded as I tuned back in. The NCAA handed out a season's suspension for steroid use. I would be a senior before I could skate again.

Skating is my life. It defines me. It earns me my father's love. It connects me to Luke.

"… a test. Okay. Also, counseling is important and mandatory at Owatonna U, okay?"

"Huh?"

"Scott, are you listening to me? We'll do a test, make this official. That is the way it has to be."

"Uh-huh," I answered. The pain in my head matched the sickness roiling in my stomach.

"Okay, we need to get a student rep—"

The door slammed open.

"What the hell is going on!" My dad was there, a bristling bear of righteous indignation.

"Mr. Caldwell, please take a seat."

This sure was official; normally Coach called my dad Gordy. They were even halfway to being friends. Not a stretch when Dad had bought the team a bus and was our volunteer driver for away games.

Will he still do that if I'm not on the team?

"Coach, all men fight. It's part of the game, and I won't support you benching him."

Wow, finally a glimmer of support from Dad, which meant absolutely nothing to me, as I sat there sweating and sick.

"Mr. Caldwell—"

"He's your star player right now."

"He's not well," Coach said.

"He's got a temper is all. About time he showed it on the ice. Scott, we're going home." Dad pulled at my jersey. "Let Coach cool down and think about this."

I didn't want to go to what Dad called home. It was nothing like home; it was a mausoleum steeped in memories of Luke. Nothing more than a box where I kept the fear, pain and shame I carried with me every day. I tried to telegraph a message to Coach without Dad seeing. *Don't make me go home with him.*

"Scott was found in possession of restricted steroids, Androstenedione, to be exact." Coach picked up the tub from the table.

Dad stopped his blustering, went bone-white, and for a moment I thought he was going to keel over and die on the spot.

"What?"

"Scott has self-reported steroid use, tests will be done, and he'll sit out the rest of the season."

Dad's defense of his angry fighting macho son vanished in an instant, horror turning into a blank expression I knew so well.

Here it comes.

"You're…" He couldn't finish the sentence, but in my head, I knew how it went. *You're nothing like Luke.* His meaning was always clear— you're not the son I wanted, not like the one I loved. "Drugs?"

"Dad—"

"You weren't even real?" He lurched back, his hand on the latch of the door.

"I just wanted…"

"I can't do this. I won't watch another son die."

He didn't listen, wrenching the door open and slamming it shut behind himself so hard the wall shook, and Coach and I were alone. Compassion flooded Coach's expression, and I wanted to cry. I wanted to sob my heart out and have Coach make it all better, ripping away all the dark bits inside me and tossing them away. Because no one else could help, and I couldn't help myself. Losing Luke had broken everything in my life, and now I had nothing left. Not even hockey.

If you don't have hockey, then you don't have a fear of your dad hating you for failing.

The next hour was a blur—tests, avoiding the team, refusing to talk to Ben, sending my apologies in words through Coach. The team was worried, or so Coach said. They wanted to see me. They were *sorry.* Sorry about what, I didn't know. None of this was their fault—I'd done this to myself.

"I'm taking you home," Coach said. He'd been with me the entire time, the student rep less happy about working with a druggie who cheated at hockey. Or at least that was what I read into her sour expression. Who could blame her? I was cheating, and I was taking banned meds. She was right.

We left the building, the arena empty, none of the guys waiting this long, no fans and students milling around, just the scent of hot dogs in the air from the closed-up carts. Empty rinks are eerie affairs, but at least no one would see my shame as I left.

There was one car in the parking lot, my dad's, and for a second a wild hope uncurled inside me. Was he here to hug me, tell me it was all going to be okay, that he wanted to be my dad again, and that he forgave me everything?

"Dad's here," I said to Coach, who gave me one final arm squeeze.

"I'll talk to you tomorrow, okay? You have my cell number. Use it. We need to get counseling organized; it's mandatory, you remember that."

"I do."

"I'm sorry I didn't see. If it was me who put pressure on you..." he began, but I didn't want a speech where blame was laid. I'd done this to myself, and I didn't really know why.

I shrugged off his touch. "It's all on me." I was good at this lying shit.

Rounding the car where Dad stood in the cold, I saw he had his thick coat wrapped around himself. I waited for him to say something, and then as Coach's car headlights swept our way, I noticed the case at his side—my case.

"I can't do this with you," Dad said and nudged at a case with his foot. "You're a cheating lying drug addict, and I don't want to *see* you."

"Dad—"

He held up a hand. "How could you do this to me? To us?"

That was always his go-to question. *How can you not be Luke* is what he really meant.

"I needed you to listen to me," I shouted. The drugs had been so good at leaving me disconnected from the world of guilt and failure that consumed me.

"Why? This will kill your mom."

"I doubt that," I snapped before I could stop myself and never saw his hand move until it connected with my face, the slap hard and full of hate. I saw tears in his eyes. I wanted to hug him. I wanted him to listen to me.

I wanted my dad.

He climbed into his car without another word and didn't look back at his only living son. Everything had crashed spectacularly. I'd hurt my best friend, my steroid abuse had been exposed, I'd earned a year's suspension, and fuck knows where I would go now. I was lost, alone, homeless, and I probably had all my worldly possessions in a suitcase and I still couldn't cry. I didn't have that emotion inside me. I was as frozen as the ice I skated on.

Hockey wasn't in my immediate future. Neither was a home. And standing there, bundled up against the cold, I was shocked, horrified, and exhausted.

But mostly I was relieved.

TWO

Hayne
_____

THE SKY REQUIRED PURPLE. A TOUCH, RIGHT WHERE THE
jagged edges of the skyline kissed the night. The brush
gathered a dollop from the top of the palette table, moving
as if it were a living thing, the synthetic hog hair bristles
releasing just the right amount of plum to the ebony I'd
applied just a moment ago. The strokes melded perfectly,
giving me the shade of midnight summer sky that I'd
envisioned when I'd woken up with this picture in my
mind an hour ago. It was a small oil, a nightscape of an
imaginary city, nothing as large or bold as I used to paint,
but it was a start.

I took a few steps back from the old porcelain-topped
table Mimi had found for me at a garage sale ten years
ago. The top was covered with fresh oil colors—blues,
purples, golds, and of course black. I never used a
handheld palette. It was either this table or my hands. The
bigger works, the ones that covered walls, were always
done by feel. The colors were too big for a simple brush.

The wall oils had to be connected hand to canvas, for them to be right.

I tipped my head to the left, trying to see where the first silver skyscraper would go. Long, brown curls fell over my eyes. Blowing them away, I moved around my attic studio, reveling in the fact that I'd woken at midnight with the urge to paint something not mired in sadness. It had been far too long.

Barefooted, I stood at the easel, my sleep pants sliding down. I yanked them up with fingers coated with azure and ebony. The painting waited as my third eye searched for the inspiration to go further. Mimi had been the first person to tell me about the third eye, or the inner eye some called it. It was an esoteric concept to be sure, but my grandmother believed. She said that creatives all had a third eye, one that witnessed the human condition and retold it through words, music, or paint. Mimi had it. My mother did too. Mimi played violin. Mom wrote poetry. Supposedly, the Ritter blessing only passed to females. I could trace creative women as far back in my family tree as I could climb. Healers, authors, artists, poets, musicians. Then there was Hayne. Maybe the Fates thought, since I was this skinny, gay kid who hid behind the headful of wild curls and was lacking most masculine traits like size and aggression, I was feminine enough to bless with the eye. The Fates were bogged down in gender norms, it seemed.

The sky wasn't right. It was missing life. I closed my eyes, the floor cold beneath my bare feet, and let myself see the city in my mind. The music playing out of my paint-speckled old stereo helped me touch the scene as I'd dreamed it. Mozart's *Concerto No. 21 in C Major* bounced off the tongue-and-groove walls of the third floor of the old rental house. I'd grown up with classical music. It was as much a part of me as oil and turpentine were. Mimi teased that she'd played the greats while Mom was pregnant to ensure the precious babe inside her daughter would have an appreciation for the arts. It must've worked. I lived and breathed music and painting.

The first hard thud on the door scared me. My eyes flew open, and the shiny silver city of my dreams disappeared into the ether. *Pop!* Like the dream that had spawned it, the vision was gone.

"Ritter! You fucking freak! It's ten after one in the fucking morning. I have an abstract algebra test tomorrow. Turn that shit down, or I will come in there and cram whatever stupid painting you're creating up your sparkly ass!"

"Sorry," I shouted, then ran across the bare wooden floor to turn off the stereo. My roommate Craig thundered back down the stairs to the second floor.

I lived up here, in the attic, and rented the rooms out below to help cover tuition and food. Craig and Dexter were this year's roomies. I tended to drive people away, for some reason. Mimi and Mom said those without the inner eye were uncouth tools who didn't deserve artistic friends. Craig was a math guy and Dexter a football player. Both were straight and found no use for the arts at all. They hated my music, my paintings, and my homosexuality. Their phobia was worse when they were mad at me. I tried not to push people. Or talk to people because when I talked to them, I somehow made them mad. Then they called me names or pushed me into walls or shoved me into lockers. Being the artsy introvert wasn't exactly fun. Even now in college, with only half a semester left before I graduated, I was still the wallflower. I hated it but knew of no way to overcome being a shy freak who smelled like citrus turpentine.

Knowing the spurt of creativity was over, I cleaned my brushes and the top of my palette table, the soft sounds of sleet hitting the massive skylights drawing my attention. I hadn't heard the storm when I'd woken up. After washing my hands in the small sink in the corner, I turned off the overhead lights with a flick of a switch and then slid into my bed. It sat in the middle of the room, surrounded by oils, easels, and my palette table. On clear nights I could see the stars and the moon. During the day, sunlight streamed through, giving me the perfect natural light to paint. Tonight, the thick panes of glass were coated with small balls of ice. I wriggled into the thick mattress and pulled the down comforter Mom had given me as a freshman up to my chin.

The pitter-patter of the sleet was soothing, and I soon drifted off, waking when the alarm on my cell phone sounded. Blinking to consciousness, I saw that the skylights were covered with snow and sleet. I snuggled down into the bed, listening to my phone as it serenaded me with some beautiful violin and piano music from my studying playlist. The wintry mix made me think of Jay-Jay, and I smiled. He had loved winter weather like this. There had been a time when I couldn't smile after losing my childhood friend. That time hadn't been all that long ago. Jay-Jay had battled his leukemia hard, but it had finally taken him. That was just eight months ago, in the spring. I'd fallen into a pit of depression that had lasted the rest of that semester. When I'd gone home for the summer, Mimi and Mom had sat me down. We'd talked, we'd cried, I'd cried a lot more than they did, and they'd taken me to the doctor. She'd given me a physical and some antidepressants. She'd also strongly recommended counseling and/or grief counseling. The summer had been rough, but over time the meds had started to lighten the dark clouds inside my mind.

Mimi had told me that creatives like us were prone to feeling things more deeply than the non-creatives. That our souls were sponges, much like our hearts. That was why we could pull words and prose and music and images from deep within. And why, at times, our works took a bit of us with them. I wondered who would take the new cityscape I'd started and what part of my heart would go with it. There was plenty of heart left inside me. I'd only ever loved three people: Mimi, Mom, and my Jay-Jay. Someday, I hoped, someone would enter my life and see past the hair and the oddness to find Hayne. Sighing dreamily, warm and moderately happy, I fantasized about that man for a moment. Then the hot water pipes rattled under the floor, signaling that Dexter and Craig were up and showering. The gauzy image of my dream man slipped away. Dexter bellowed about coffee, and I yanked the cover over my head.

Willing my roommates away never worked. Soon they were thundering up and down the stairs, bitching about classes and women and whatever. I tried not to get too close to the guys who lived here with me. This house, four blocks from campus, was my refuge. My grandfather left me a small amount of money for school, but my talent had won me grants and scholarships, so the tuition was covered. Books, food, clothes, and incidentals were not. I'd used his money to rent the house outright, the contract was mine, but that wasn't financially sustainable and I had finally been forced to share my space. It went against my hermit nature, but I had to eat. And buy paint and canvas. God knows the pittance I made working in a little coffee shop in the basement of the English department building didn't cover much.

"Hey, Ritter, you got any soap stashed in there?" Dexter shouted through the crack in the door. "Hey. I need soap. Craig used it all. Ritter! Wake up!"

"Right, okay." I ran to my wardrobe, found a bar of green soap, and padded reluctantly to the door. Unlocking it carefully, I cracked it open and looked up at the mountain of defensive end staring down at me. "Here. It's the last bar I have, so can you replace it. Please?"

"Yep. Thanks." He flashed me a killer grin, patted my head, and jogged down the narrow stairs, whistling some stupid song.

"Note to self. Buy soap," I said as I closed the door.

TWO DAYS LATER, I was making my usual dash from the tiny art department building to the financial aid building. My head was down, my hair whipping my face, snow and wind blowing over the campus with the latest Canadian locomotive cold front. Winter in Minnesota was fun. Dying of exposure moving from class to class was a real possibility. I struggled with the door, the wind swirling around the old brick building so violently it ripped my scarf off and carried it to the heavens. Probably Thor's goats now had them a cute pinkish-purple scarf to play with. We were in Minnesota. Viking heritage ruled.

"Hey! Hold that door!" I glanced over my shoulder, and a huge guy came barreling at me through the blizzard. "Christ, what the hell is with this stupid snow?"

He pushed around me, his dark hair coated with snowflakes, as were the shoulders of his athletic jacket. A gust hit me in the face. I stumbled back into him, my eyes and nose packed full of snow.

"Step aside." He nudged to the left and gave a mighty yank on the door. Even with his size and strength it was a chore to get it open wide enough for us to wiggle in. He shoved me inside as I was still sputtering and wiping at my face. He slipped through sideways, his shoulders far too wide to enter normally.

I stumbled into the foyer of the financial aid office. He rushed in behind me, shaking his head like a wet dog. Melting snow flew in my face. I mumbled under my breath and turned away from the jock. That was my usual modus operandi with athletes. Putting as much space between his fist and my face as possible. There was something about a puny artist that just brought out the bully in his type.

"You're lucky you didn't blow away with your scarf. Here." I looked back at him slowly. He had my scarf in his hand. "I had to backtrack nearly to the science building to catch it."

"Oh, uhm, thanks." I took it from him gently, my movements slow, in case he decided to snap it back or hold it over my head and make me jump for it. I wrapped the cold and soaking wet scarf Mimi had knitted for me around my neck.

"You know where the grief counseling group meets?"

I blinked up at him. He was beautiful in a classic way. Dark hair, incredible bone structure, hazel eyes that burned with a sadness only few could recognize. He smiled, but there was no joy in his grin.

"Second floor," I replied, wishing he was less attractive or less manly or less pained. "There are rooms up there. The LGBT Coalition I go to also meets up there every Thursday."

My eyes flared when I realized what I'd said. So now he knew I was a rainbow guy and would either slowly creep away or deck me for admiring his bone structure.

"Yeah? Huh. I didn't know they had one of those here."

I lowered my chin so my nose and mouth were covered with sodden scarf. He had a Grecian nose, long and straight. I had to say something.

"It's a group for gay people."

Ah, brilliant, Hayne. Well done! Clap, clap. Shall we just sprout rainbow wings and fart glitter to ensure the football player pounds you into mush?

"I kind of figured." He hefted a big bag up onto his shoulder and yanked at a case on wheels. "You here for grief counseling?" I nodded. He studied me for a minute. "Mandated?"

"Voluntary," I mumbled into my scarf. Was it possible that the yarn still smelled like sheep? Was that me? I hoped not. I'd bought and used soap. Daily.

"Oh, hey sorry about the smell." He hoisted the bag up higher. "My hockey gear is in here."

Hockey. Not football. The sport where they beat people up with wooden sticks. Super. Time for the queer arty guy to make a hasty exit.

"I'm heading up." I jerked a thumb at the elevator.

"Mind if I ride up with you? This is my first time and we kind of know each other so…" He let it dangle. I wasn't sure that a shared door battle really made us bosom buddies. Still, he *did* run after and return my scarf, and he was the most beautiful man I had ever seen in all my twenty-two years. And he did possess the saddest eyes I'd ever seen. All of that was too much for my spongy heart to take.

"Sure. Okay."

I spun around and walked to the elevator, my arms cinched around my middle. He came up beside me.

"My name is Scott, in case you were wondering."

"Hayne."

The doors slid open, and we stepped inside. Then we both turned to face forward. I hugged myself more tightly and kept my eyes on the floor panel. There were only three, so the ride went quickly.

The bag on his shoulder really smelled bad. I wanted to pinch my nose, but he might've taken offense to that.

The *ping* sounded, and a push of fresh, warm air rushed into the elevator. I scurried into the corridor, glanced up and down the hall, and then saw where the student counselor was this week. The office changed, depending on who was still at work in financial aid. Today, lots of staff had left early because of the winter weather dumping snow on the region.

"Down here," I said. He followed me, looking uneasy. We got to the open door, and the aroma of coffee met us like a long-lost neighbor. "You might want to leave that bag out here."

"No, can't do that. All my gear is in it. My skates and pads. You know how expensive those are?"

"No," I said and shook my head. Several damp curls fell over my left eye. I blew at them, but they were too wet to fly, so I shoved them behind my ear.

"Well, they're really expensive, and I'm really broke, so they go where I go."

"Okay." I wasn't going to press the point. I walked into the room and gave Monica, the student counselor or therapist, whichever term worked, a smile and a wave. She was a nice woman, older and pudgy, with brown hair and a caring smile. I'd been coming to this group since the semester had started and found it really helpful. Lots of kids on campus took advantage of the groups and on-campus therapist. Not just for grief, but for other things like stress, anxiety, and support dealing with addictions. That was a different group, but I knew a few kids from the small shop where I worked, who went and raved about how it was helping them with the fight to stay clean.

I sat on a chair, buried my nose in my scarf, and pulled my legs into my chest. Scott gave the small group a look that screamed trepidation, but to his credit, he lowered his ass into the chair beside me, dropped his foul bag to the floor between us, and began working on his lower lip.

"Hello, everyone, my name is Monica. Looks like we have a small group tonight. That's fine, makes it cozier." Monica gave us all a happy little smile. "Since we're freshly back from the Christmas break, let's talk a bit about how we dealt with the loss of our loved ones during the holidays. This is always a difficult time when we're working through our grief. Would anyone like to go first?" She studied the skinny black girl on my left, then me. I hid inside my scarf. I never went first. Ever. "How about our new member? Why don't you tell us who you are and how your holiday season was?"

We all turned to look at Scott.

THREE

Scott
―――――

EVERYONE TURNED TO STARE AT ME, AND I'D NEVER FELT
more exposed.

I'd burned a hell of a lot of bridges to get to this point.
The last two weeks had been the longest of my life. I
hadn't seen Ben yet. He'd visited home for Christmas, and
he hadn't contacted me over the holidays or come to find
me since he'd come back. He'd texted me a couple of
times since New Year, but I wasn't ready to see that I'd
destroyed our friendship, and apart from the first line that
showed on my preview screen, I didn't read the rest and
deleted them immediately. Same as I did for several
messages from the rest of the Eagles.

What they wanted to say to me could stay unseen until
they talked to me and I could face their accusations
head on.

I knew for certain Ben was back at college because
I'd seen him heading into the rink, along with Jacob and
Ryker. I got the message. I'd fucked up big-time,
probably left him with a vicious scar, and lost another

friend along the way. Nothing more than I deserved, really.

I wondered if Ryker was angry with me as well. We'd become friends in the summer, and he had my number. What if I spoke to him? Maybe I could crash at his and Jacob's place.

In their tiny dorm room, with the pushed-together beds. Yeah, right.

Jacob had texted me five times, wanting to talk apparently, then saying in his last terse message that he was there if I needed him. At least one of the team cared, I guess, and he did sign the first one I'd actually read from him and Ryker both. Coach was still in touch, but I was pulling away, from him, from hockey, from the team, from it all. In fact, I was shoving all my hopes and dreams into a box that I wasn't planning on opening ever again.

And now this group of strangers wanted me to tell them how I'd spent my Christmas?

I'd used up my savings getting a cheap motel room. That summed up what I'd done for Christmas. That, and buying a charger for my phone because Dad hadn't packed mine. I had the sum total of thirty-seven dollars and twenty-three cents left in my bank, and even though I'd picked up shifts at work, I wasn't pulling in enough to cover rent anywhere. I needed to get to the rink in town and see if they had any kid coaching positions, or hell, I'd sweep up after parties and events. Anything for money.

No parent will want you anywhere near their kids, you fucking idiot.

The only silver lining was that Dad had set up a trust to pay all four years of my tuition, used it as a tax write-off, so I didn't have to leave college. *Even if I do end up sleeping on a bench in the middle of a Minnesota winter, just to be able to stay and study.* I shuddered at the thought and glanced out of the window at the sleet and hail smashing against the glass. I knew the college had emergency housing they could give me for a few days, but it was never intended for a long-term situation and certainly not for enough time to get through to the end of the year, not to mention the remaining time with my chemistry degree. When I had that degree, I could do anything, but even that had been slipping from my grasp, slowly but surely, as I fucked up assignments and had nearly burned down the lab during my last practical.

I died a little more inside when I cast a look at the people waiting for me to talk, and my gaze snapped to Hayne's. His eyes were the color of chocolate, and I lost myself in them for a moment until he blushed and glanced away.

Those same eyes had shown fear at first until he'd found out that I was heading for the same place as him. I thought he'd seen nothing but a jock when he'd met me, and I'd noticed that reaction from some of the students on campus before. I wasn't small. Hell, compared to Hayne I was a giant, and he might've known me, and may even have heard about my aggression at the last game. It seemed like a lot of people on campus had heard about my steroid abuse and me losing my shit if the pointed looks I received were anything to go by. I wondered if the concept of me going to a grief group made me feel as less of a threat to him. All I knew was that there was compassion in his velvet eyes. I cleared my throat and waited for words to come to me.

What exactly had I done for Christmas and how could I explain without having to elaborate?

"The usual," I finally offered. If usual was eating Cheetos and drinking water for Christmas dinner or watching the ball drop on a crappy TV that kept fizzing and popping as it tried desperately to show me colors.

Monica, the leader of this group, was a motherly type; an older woman, all soft and cuddly around the edges, with brown hair. She sent me an encouraging smile, and I knew she wanted more from me. Hell, shouldn't I be breaking down right now, sobbing out my story, about how my brother died, how it was my fault, how my dad couldn't look at me, how my mom was a ghost in her own house? Wasn't *that* what they wanted to hear?

None of those words made it out of my head, and so the turn passed to the girl sitting next to me, dressed from head to toe in black, with thick kohl-rimmed eyes and an angry expression. Obviously I wasn't the only one who didn't want to be here.

"I hate this mandatory shit," she snapped and tugged her sleeves down, drawing attention as she did to the marks on her wrists. She pulled at the threads that were stark against her pale skin, and I tried not to stare. It was all I could do to stop myself from offering my fist to bump in agreement. Seeing a private counselor after Luke's death had been bad enough, but being forced to sit in a room with other people and talk about myself? That was hell.

Goth-girl sighed heavily. "Okay, whatever." It soon became obvious that the angry attitude wasn't just an act. "I'm Alice. Yes, it's after the book, and yes, I hate it. Mom had breast cancer, stage four. She died on Christmas Eve last year. Dad lost his shit, ended up being committed. I went to an aunt who was a real bitch, always on my back, but Dad came home early December, and I spent Christmas with him." The whole monologue spilled out in what seemed like a single breath. "So yeah, it was a blast, and it's not like I fucking give a shit about any of them." She air quoted the words, and I suspected her Christmas had been as awful as mine.

I waited for her to add something, but she deliberately turned to the boy sitting next to her with a very loud, "Next!"

The student was startled, jumped in his seat, and I recognized him as a fellow science major, physics I think, very clever, normally wore glasses.

"I'm Oscar, uhm... I spent Christmas with my mom and my brothers. We had our cousins over, my grandparents. It was a good Christmas, no time to think about missing Dad at all." He stared down at his hands and added a wistful, "No time at all."

There was silence then, and we all looked expectantly at Hayne, who sat, back straight and chin tilted defiantly. He was really something, with his head of messy curly hair that appeared so soft, and those gorgeous eyes brimming with emotion. He'd spoken about the "gay" thing as if I might want to know, and he'd never met me before. I wasn't exactly out and proud, but I loved whom I loved. I know the proper label is bisexual, but living under Dad's roof, that was a word we didn't use. I'd lost the one person who'd understood my sexuality. My brother. Luke wasn't just my brother; he'd been my friend and confidant.

Hayne still wasn't talking, and I wondered what the

protocol was at this point. Should the baton skip him? Or what?

"Hi, I'm Hayne. I spent Christmas with Mimi and Mom," he began, and his tone was soft, melodic, full of happiness. I guess everyone else knew who Mimi was because he didn't elaborate for my sake. "We had a really good Christmas Day, but..." He tilted his chin again, and I wondered if maybe he was working through whatever his grief was with sheer grit and determination. "New Year's Day was hard because that was always our day, mine and Jay-Jay's, and I felt incredibly alone, and the meds didn't seem to want to help me. But then, on January second, it was easier."

A lot of people nodded as if they agreed with what he was saying, that after Christmas and New Year was done, it was all so much easier.

We went around the room, all five of us saying something, and then we were back to me, and I didn't *have* to say anything, but I thought I should because everyone else there had shared a small part of themselves, and I kind of wanted to say something.

"Okay then. So my name is Scott. I'm a hockey player with the Eagles, or at least I was until before Christmas." I glanced around to see if anyone recognized me or my name, or hell, even hockey. Not one person showed anything but polite interest. "I self-reported for steroid abuse. I wanted... hell, I don't know what I wanted... but it wasn't any more of a life without my brother, where I did nothing but fuck things up, and where my home life was strained." I cleared my throat, as the words were all bunched up and stuck there. "So yeah, Christmas sucked."

The leader smiled at me, all compassion and

understanding, and I couldn't help myself. I bristled. That set the tone for the rest of the meeting. We talked about coping strategies, academia, and cats. A hell of a lot about cats, which seemed to be goth-girl's way of coping.

Maybe I need to get a cat. Where would a cat live? In a box with me?

The meeting ended at eight, and I left just as quickly as everyone else, all apart from the kid called Oscar, who wanted to talk to Monica alone.

"You stink," Alice announced as she passed me.

"It's my bag," I defended, but she wrinkled her nose and scurried ahead. She wasn't making herself very likable with her prickly in-your-face attitude.

"Ignore her," Hayne said from my side. "She's not always like that, but holidays suck, right?"

I made a general noise of agreement and hoisted my huge bag over my shoulder, pulling the case on wheels with me.

"You going somewhere?" Hayne asked.

"In between places," I said and didn't add anything else, but the look he gave me was thoughtful.

"We should get coffee," he tugged at his scarf, hiding half his face again. I know we're about to go out into a storm, but I really wished he didn't hide his lips. He pushed back the long curls that fell across his forehead with an impatient huff, then unrolled the scarf. Were we not going outside then, or had he understood my unspoken wish? "This way." He headed down the corridor away from the exit. I had two choices. The first was heading out into the storm with nowhere to go; the second was to follow Hayne.

The cute and sexy guy was the lesser of two evils. That

was all it was, so I went after him, and finally we were in a back room, without windows but with a working coffee machine. I knew where we must be. It was obvious from the rainbow flags, the notices about sexual health, the posters about love and support. The entire room was a kaleidoscope of color.

Hayne dropped gracefully to his knees, rummaged under a desk, his ass in the air, and I had to stop myself from saying something inappropriate, as any jock would.

"Aha!" Hayne said and pulled out a Tupperware container with a flourish. "Leftover Christmas cookies. You want?"

Given I'd eaten nothing since breakfast, the idea of anything resembling food was a very good thing. He passed the box to me, and I peeled the lid open. Inside, Santas nestled next to angels, and snowmen were stacked next to three Rudolph cookies. These could've fed me for two days, but I didn't take them all. I very carefully selected two Santa cookies iced in scarlet, white, and black. They were the biggest. I nibbled on one and watched Hayne poke at the coffee machine, pressing buttons and muttering under his breath, until with a triumphant smile, he passed me a white coffee.

"I hope you like creamer because we didn't have any black coffee capsules left. Hermione said she'd get some, but she's kinda flaky. Last time we sent her out for sugar, she came back with a bag of rice."

"Rice?"

He grinned ruefully. "Don't ask."

"With cream is great," I said and inhaled the scent of the wonder that was hot caffeine. I finished off the second cookie, sipped at the coffee, and all that time Hayne was staring at me. At first, I caught his gaze and met it head on, and then I couldn't look at him, because he was staring at me with a hundred questions in his expression.

Not a good thing when I didn't have any answers.

"So, where are you going?" he asked and gestured at my bags. "What's in those apart from foul-smelling but expensive hockey stuff?"

I could've lied, told him nothing, kept everything to myself, but he was harmless, curled up on the sofa in front of me, a rainbow on the wall behind him framing his face and his soft curls.

"I don't fucking know where I'm going, okay? I'm out of money, and I've fucked everything up so much that my friends aren't my friends anymore, and I don't even have a place to stay." My words were aggressive, and he winced as they spat out at him. He sipped his coffee, then deliberately placed his angel cookie on his knee and hesitated for a moment before sighing.

"Nowhere?" he asked softly.

I shook my head, and the tears stuck in my chest made me press a hand to my heart at the pain. "Dad kicked me out."

"Because you're gay?"

"I'm not gay," I snapped, and he did that whole wincing thing again. I honestly think he expected me to launch myself over and attack him right there and then. "I'm bi." Saying the words out loud to someone other than Ben or my brother was weird. The shape of the words felt foreign to me, but I was only telling the truth.

He smiled then, a soft smile, and picked up the angel cookie to eat some more. "So they kicked you out for being bi?"

"No." I huffed a laugh and helped myself to a Rudolph and another fat Santa. "Mom doesn't even care who I am anymore, and Dad? He's all about the way people see our family, and it was okay while I did what he said, as long as I tried to make him proud and aimed to be a mini-Luke. But when I decided to stop doing that, and believe me, I did it in spectacular fashion, he was done with me." I pointed at the bags. "That's all of it," I said. "Everything I own or at least everything he thought I'd need."

"Is Luke your brother?"

I nodded because the words hurt too much to say.

"And you lost him?"

"I hate that term," I said tiredly and slid down in the comfortable chair. "I didn't lose him. It's not as if I'll ever find him one day. He drowned."

"I'm sorry. To lose a brother, I can't imagine."

I had to know more details of why Hayne was at the group. I couldn't help myself. "Was it one of your family who died?"

"No, my closest friend, leukemia, six months ago."

"I'm sorry for your loss." And I was because it made his soft smile slip to think about his friend.

He concentrated on the cookie, but there was so much pain in him, and I wanted to reach for his hand and reassure him. I didn't because I wasn't sure if it'd be welcomed at all, and I was all out of being pushed away by people. He glanced up and tilted his chin, just as he had in the meeting.

"Look, Scott, I know this is going to sound weird, but I have somewhere you can stay for a while. It's not much, and you'd have to put up with…" He waved his hand at himself, and God knows what that meant. "It's yours if you want it."

I stopped mid-bite, Santa's head remaining intact for the time being. "What?"

"In my house, you can have a mattress on the floor if it helps. We have a shower and a washing machine. You can stay."

"You don't know me." I couldn't help the disapproval in my voice. He was too vulnerable to be offering a place to a total stranger.

He looked right into me. "Grief knows grief, and I want to help."

I was lost, and he was an angel offering me space on his floor. There wasn't anything else I could say. I wasn't stupid.

"Thank you."

FOUR

Hayne

_____

*WHAT HAVE YOU DONE? WHAT HAVE YOU DONE? HAYNE,
what have you done?*

The walk to my house in the howling winter storm was
brutal and slow. The sidewalks were coated with slippery
sleet and snow, which made walking difficult. The wind
was bitterly cold and scoured any exposed flesh. My nose
ran, and my eyes watered. Scott, somehow, kept pushing
onward, shoulders up, his face, head, and neck exposed to
the brutal weather. Ice particles clung to his long, dark
lashes. I pulled off my mittens—they were mates to the
purple-pink scarf—and offered them to him about two
blocks into the walk. He shook his head, dislodging about
an inch of snow. A sudden urge to towel off his hair, then
blow it dry overtook me. Maybe sit him over the old-
fashioned metal grate in the hardwood floor that blew hot
air into the attic. Cover him with that dark rose blanket
Mimi had made for my bed two years ago. Feed him some
of the tuna salad in my dorm fridge and offer him a glass
of lemon-lime soda or some corn chips. Perhaps he would

smile at me, and we'd cuddle under the soft knitted coverlet as the storm rattled the skylights.

"… more than me."

A gust roared around the corner of Blue Bonnet Drive, hurling snow and tiny bits of ice into our faces.

"Take them. I have a scarf," I yelled to be heard over the whipping wind.

He shook his head and crammed his hands deeper into the pockets of his varsity jacket.

I sighed in defeat and trudged on, slipping off the curb as I went to cross the street. Scott helped keep me steady, his fingers biting into my biceps.

"… careful."

I nodded at the garbled warning, picturing his words being ripped from him and carried skyward to Ullr, the Norse god of snow and skiing. Man, skis would be nice…

We plowed onward, his elbow rapping mine with every step, as if he were staying close in case I fell or was lifted heavenward as his words had been. Knowing he was there was nice.

"That's my place," I shouted as we joined Periwinkle Lane. The houses were older on this block, like mine, and probably fifty percent were rentals housing OU students. He shucked his bag higher on his shoulders, and gave me a curt nod. Stepping into the ratty foyer of my house had never felt better. We both sighed at the blast of warmth enveloping us.

"That was the longest four blocks ever," Scott grumbled, his cheeks windburned and bright red, his hair and eyebrows frozen. I stamped my feet to knock the snow off my boots. Scott did the same.

"The lease is in my name, and my room is up there." I

pointed up the stairs that climbed to the second floor. "Down here is the living room, laundry room, and kitchen. Second floor has two bedrooms which are my roommates', and we're in the attic. Oh, and the bathroom is on the second floor, but I suggest you use the corner shower and toilet in my studio. My roommates don't believe in cleaning. Anything."

"Noted."

We peeled off our wet coats and draped them on hooks by the door. Boots were placed on a boot tray to dry. Scarves and mittens were hung over the railing.

I was just starting up the stairs when Dexter came thundering down on the heels of a young woman in a bra and skirt. She shrieked and giggled and bounced around me and Scott. Dexter paused midway down the stairs, his attention riveted on the burly hockey player standing behind me.

"I know you," Dexter said. I glanced back at Scott. My guest seemed uneasy, his eyebrows knotting up slightly. "Did we meet at that party Ken Inver threw when semester started?"

"Uh, I don't know. Maybe," Scott muttered. I tried to move around Dexter, but he simply put a hand on my head and held me in place. I hated it when people did that. Damn jocks.

And yet you've invited one to sleep in your sacred space. What have you done?

"Yeah, it was you. Man, you were all sorts of fucked up. Took a swing at Lonkowski," Dexter said with a grin.

"Sorry, I don't remember." Scott was so distant now, his speech cold as the night we'd just come in from.

"No, I bet not. You were a wreck," Dexter said, slapping Scott on the shoulder in praise.

Did he really look up to another person for getting drunk or high? I'd never taken drugs, aside from my meds, in my life. My escape was found on the canvas. Maybe Scott needed to find a better way to cope. Maybe I could teach him to paint.

The girl shouted for Dexter to come find her. His dark eyes lit up. "Looks like we both found someone to spend a long, cold night with, huh, Ritter?" Dexter asked, gave me a playful punch in the arm that hurt way more than I let on, and then raced around us in pursuit of his latest conquest.

That was just another reason why I hid in the attic. Squeals of passion from drunken sorority girls all night long made me queasy and itchy.

We climbed the narrow staircase in wet socks, making a left at the top. "Those are the bedrooms. I'm not allowed in them."

Scott blinked at me in confusion. "What happens if you go into their rooms?"

I rubbed my biceps in reply. Scott's brows tangled more deeply.

With him on my heels, I climbed one more flight of creaky stairs. The door to the attic was heavy and rested on amazing brass hinges that I oiled regularly. Stepping inside, I then reached to the left and threw on the overhead lights.

"Wow," I heard Scott murmur.

I smiled to myself. "You can drop your bags in the corner over there, open them up, and we'll do something with your gear. The shower stall, sink, and toilet are behind that curtain." I jogged around my bed in the middle of the floor and tugged on the long white curtain that Mom had installed for me when I'd moved in nearly four years ago. We'd paid the landlord to put a small bath up there for me. I had some issues with sharing bathrooms, stemming from several bad incidents in high school that had taken place in locker rooms. I reached up to gather my hair into a ponytail and held it in place. The curtain rings rolled around the pipe we'd installed. "Soap and shampoo are on that shelf. Towels on the corner rack."

"Nice," he said, standing under the skylights, his head tipped back, his thick neck exposed. "These are cool."

"Ah, yeah, you can see the stars."

He glanced at me over my bed. "Let it down."

"What?"

"Your hair. It looks cute down. In your face." Heat raced up my neck to my cheeks. I slowly released the curls. Fourteen or so sprang forward and covered my right eye. "Yeah, that's super cute." He seemed flustered, as if the words hadn't meant to leave his mouth at all.

After that, I had trouble talking to him. He patrolled my space, his bags on the floor by my bed, studying all the oils on the walls or stacked in the corners. The one I'd started a few days ago was still on the easel.

"This looks like Manhattan," he said, touching the canvas lightly as if he expected the paint to be wet. I took two cans of lemon-lime soda out of my fridge and offered him one. He took it but never opened it. "Is that where you grew up?"

"No, I'm from Rhode Island. That's just a mindscape, a city of imagination." I walked to my bed and sat on it, drawing my knees to my chest, then wiggling my cold toes in my wet socks. "I dreamed it."

"Yeah?" He stared at me and then at the half-finished painting. "I never dream of stuff like that."

"What do you dream of?" I popped the tab on my soda and took a long swig. The sugar would probably keep me up, but that was okay. Maybe Scott would want to stay up to tell me my curls were cute again.

"Nothing. I dream of nothing. Can I shower now?"

I bobbed my head. He went to the corner, yanked the white curtain around him, sealing him off from me and my stupid questions.

I drank the whole can of soda in one long pull, belched, and then hurried to change while the water was running. Once my sleep pants were up over my backside, I draped my damp clothes over a wooden clothes-drying rack by the grate in the floor. Steam billowed out of the curtained-off area, the moist air rich with the smell of my citrus body wash. I rushed to pull an old air mattress out of the closet, and using a bike pump, I worked on blowing it up for him.

After the mattress was inflated, I dug into an old trunk of Mimi's that was packed full with bedding. Clean sheets and a nice warm crocheted cover should make him comfy. I wanted him warm and dry as he slept. I glanced at the corner. He was going to drain the hot water heater, and then my roommates would be mad. Mad roommates were a bad thing.

He still wasn't done washing when I'd gotten his bed set up, so I crawled into mine and waited, my heart thundering wildly.

What have you done?

"I don't know," I whispered to myself, but whatever I'd done, it was going to be something that changed my life. I could feel it, as if the cosmos was subtly realigning in some ethereal way that would forever change my existence. Or the sugar from the soda was kicking in.

"Where do we hang the towels?"

I looked at him and instantly regretted it. He was far too masculine, standing there in fleece pants and a gray tank top, his hair rumpled from a firm toweling, and his shoulders still damp from the lengthy shower. My fingers itched to touch each droplet, remove it from his skin, and take it onto my tongue so I could taste him.

Scott held up his wet towel. My dick stirred in my sleep pants.

"On that rack," I whispered, then burrowed deeper into my covers, leaving just my eyes peeking out. He was beautiful. Muscled, strong, and lost. So obviously lost. "Can you turn off the lights before you get into bed?"

I didn't dare leave my mattress with a raging hard-on.

"Sure." He made his way to the switch after hanging up his towel. The lights went out with a faint *snap*. I rolled to my side so I could observe him, even though it was now dark in the attic. The nightlight beside the toilet was hidden behind the privacy curtain, but I knew when he found the air mattress. It groaned under his weight. Just as I would…

And my cock just got even harder. Super.

"Hey uh, Hayne?" he said a few moments later. I yanked my hand out of my sleep pants at the sound of his sleepy voice.

"Yeah?"

"Thanks for this. You're… this is… thanks."

"It's okay. We all need a helping hand from time to time."

"Yeah, yeah, we do. Night."

"Goodnight."

He must have been exhausted because he dropped off instantly. Whenever I'd been in a strange place, it had taken me forever to drift off. Not Scott. He was out like the proverbial light. I lay there, my eyes closed and my ears sharp, listening to him breathe while the storm blustered and blew outside. Who knew what tomorrow would bring? Whatever it would be, I bet it wasn't going to be mundane or boring.

MY DREAMS WERE full of vintage spun glass ornaments and red stags, icy cold castles with snow-covered parapets, and a knight of winter. He rode a white horse, and his armor was silvery like a frozen lake. Blues and whites and moth grays followed me out of slumber, the skylight over me packed with snow. The wind had died down overnight. All I could hear was the water pipes leading up to the attic creaking and Scott's deep, restful breaths.

I had to paint. Not that cityscape I'd started, but something with periwinkle and slate gray, dabs of bone white and lavender. And the knight. Yes, he had to be represented as well. Maybe as a bold splash of pure white amid the swirling colors of winter. His horse could be the winter winds themselves, and his lance crafted of ice. I slid from the bed, turned on the lights, and threw the cityscape aside, my hands trembling with the rush only painting had ever given me. I pawed through drawers filled with brushes and tubes of oil, finding the cold colors my inner eye told me to use. Within minutes, the top of my palette table was covered with globs of blues, charcoal, a tender pink, some iris for the purple, and white. Lots of white.

Using a wide four-inch brush, I picked up the white and began applying it to the new canvas. I worked the paint into violent swirls, then added the pink, the brush dribbling paint to the floor and my toes. My breathing picked up as the storm on the canvas blew into existence. My mind slipped into that place where all creatives go, that world where it's only me and my art. Lost in color and texture, I grabbed the remote for my stereo and turned on some music. I skipped ahead until I found Vivaldi. I fast-forwarded through the first three seasons. *Winter* filled the room. My arms prickled with gooseflesh. I threw my hair from my face, picked up a smaller brush, and ran the bristles through some slate paint. The winter knight spoke to me.

"Is this part of your usual morning routine?"

I spun around to face Scott sitting up on his air mattress, his eyes hooded and sleepy, his neck and cheeks scruffy, and his hair sloppy from sleep. He was wearing this odd, crooked smile that made me feel lightheaded and sort of silly.

"I… was inspired," I replied, reaching for the remote to turn down the music that everyone on campus who wasn't a music student or Hayne Ritter hated. "Sorry."

"No, hey, it's cool. Leave it on." Mimi's blanket puddled in his lap. "You're cute when you're inspired."

I lowered the remote and gaped at him. He stood. I blew curls out of my face. "The music…"

"Is you." I had no words. "Go ahead and paint. Are there any classes, or did they cancel?"

"Classes?" I asked because half of Hayne was still in the land of the winter knight.

Scott laughed. It was just a short one, kind of barky but deep and appealing. "You're really adorable."

"I, uhm… you're the winter knight. He's powerful and rides a snow horse, and the North winds blow when he and his steed race across the cold skies."

Scott blinked at me.

Oh my God, Hayne, what have you done?

FIVE

Scott

"YOU'RE THE WINTER KNIGHT." HE WAS TALKING TO ME, about me?

I heard the words and blinked at Hayne, not at all sure what he wanted me to say back to him. I'd seen poetry from passion generated on the ice. I'd seen chemical reactions form prisms of color in the classroom, so I knew enough about art to be dangerous, but I'd never seen anyone construct something as Hayne had done. The choice of colors, the way his whole body swayed as he painted, and the beautiful images he was creating were a sight to see. There was paint everywhere, dripping off the canvas, down his clothes, his hands wet with it, and he was breathing heavily. Every part of him was connected to the painting, and it was possibly the sexiest thing I'd ever seen. Scratch that; it was *the* sexiest thing, bar none. I could honestly say no one had ever called me a winter knight, so I assumed it was an art thing, but my confidence slipped away. I'd started this damn conversation, and now it was up to me to carry it on.

"Oh, cool," I finally said and saw the moment the simple words disappointed him.

His expression became more guarded, and I noticed he took a step away from me. Why did that reaction cut so deep, and why did I feel I had the ability at that moment to destroy his world? I carefully sidestepped him, purposefully not crowding him at all, and peered at the painting. I felt something squelch under my foot and assumed my sock was now covered in one of the icy colors he'd used. I didn't care. Somehow nothing was as important as making him smile.

"Not just cool, I actually meant to say it's a beautiful painting, and I'm blown away that somehow I made it onto canvas." There. That would be enough, right? He'd smile again now and say something that diffused the situation.

Silence.

I turned to face him, but he wouldn't meet my eyes. Instead he fiddled with the volume control, which was rapidly turning icy-gray as the paint transferred from his hands. Yet again I had seriously fucked up, and I wanted to fix it. I reached for his hand, and he didn't stop me from taking the control, which nearly slipped from my grasp. I put the music back up, allowing the beautiful notes to fill the room. Then I placed it very carefully back onto the small table Hayne had taken it from. I tilted his chin with a finger so he had to look up at me, and for a millisecond I was lost in his soft eyes. Before I attempted to clumsily kiss him, cementing the weird electric connection we appeared to have going on, I found some words I hoped would help.

"You're so talented," I said and then released my hold and handed him the last brush he'd been using. Now all I had to do was snap him out of whatever fear or concern I'd put into him, and I did my usual Scott thing, gesturing at myself and then the painting. "I think you missed a bit," I said. Before he could say anything back, I went behind the curtain to wash my hands of the paint, only it really wasn't coming off. I probably needed some paint thinners or something. Otherwise I'd be left looking like I had ghost hands for the rest of the day, if not longer.

"You need these," Hayne murmured, coming to stand next to me and nudging dish soap and olive oil toward me. "Use a little of both, and it will get rid of the paint. They're not chemicals, so it's okay on your skin."

I put on my best smile, thanked him, and he disappeared back into the main room as I cleaned off the color. When I came out, he was lost again in painting and didn't seem at all perturbed that I was in the room watching him. There was a message about canceled classes on my phone, so at least I didn't have to go outside today, and right about now, I was very happy with that, quite content to sit on my mattress, propped up with my back to the wall, and watch Hayne work. I thought maybe I should tell Hayne about class cancelations, but I wasn't sure what building he would even be in or what he studied. Apart from art, I assumed. I didn't want to be the one to break the spell again, so I kept really quiet and checked the news instead. I didn't have the Wi-Fi password yet, so mobile data was where it was at, but that didn't matter either. Hell, nothing seemed to matter this morning. Apart from when my cell vibrated and I saw Jacob's name with a text alert, and I thumbed to my messages without thinking.

The message was certainly short and to the point.

We're done messing around. The Aviary, one hour, no excuses.

My chest tightened, my stomach sank, and there was no way in hell I wanted to go the local hangout for the Owatonna Eagles hockey team. The café was supposed to be for the entirety of the student body, but the colors and pennants on the wall were for the Owatonna Eagles hockey team. It only held about thirty people at a time and would be mostly empty this early on a school day, but still...

No way can I face Jacob.

Hayne turned to look at me, and for a moment, I thought I'd said something out loud.

"Are you okay?" Hayne asked and frowned at me.

"What?"

"You sighed really hard. I could hear it over the music."

"Nothing, just... I have friends." I stopped and then corrected myself. "I had friends. They want to see me."

"You should go." Hayne pushed at his hair, a streak of pale blue icing the tip of one persistent curl.

"They must hate me, and I don't think I'm ready to hear what they have to say," I muttered, dropped my cell to the blanket, then scrubbed at my eyes. When I opened them again, Hayne was crouching in front of me, and I reached out and brushed a curl from over his eye. He didn't flinch, but I was kind of mortified I'd gone straight for his hair like that.

"Trust me, if they're real friends, they want to see you for a reason."

I laughed, a bitter noise that startled both of us. "I let the team down, I permanently scarred my friend, I lost my shit, beat up perfect strangers, and I haven't returned anyone's texts."

Hayne nodded. "Then you go and see them now, and if you've gone too far and they pull away, then they weren't friends in the first place."

I wish I believed it would be that easy. Ben and I had been close for a long time, naturally gravitating toward each other over our love of hockey and Cheetos, and Jacob had been a constant in my life, keeping me solid and settled. But I'd made an art out of pushing people away.

"Okay." I picked up my cell and fired off a quick *I'll be there,* then regretted it as soon as I'd pressed send.

"Scott, do you need an advocate?" Hayne asked softly.

"Huh?"

The meaning of the word escaped me at first, as if I'd never even heard it before, and then the sense of everything was back, but I must have hesitated too long. Hayne looked concerned.

"Scott, do you want me to come with you?"

The offer was genuine, I could see that, but I couldn't take him into The Aviary when I didn't know what I was facing. The idea of dragging Hayne into a shouting match wasn't a good one, nor did I want Hayne to see the final strings of friendship being cut.

"I think I need to do this on my own."

"Okay, I get that, but you need to go. If I had people who potentially cared about me, I would be meeting up for coffee so fast it would make your head spin."

Something in his words made me stop. *If he had people...* Did he not have anyone? That sounded so wrong, and I wanted to tell him that...

What? That I'm here for him? Am I actually losing my

shit here? I don't even really know him, but I could be a friend if he needed one.

I didn't get to say that, and with a shy smile, he went back to his painting and left me to make a choice.

THE AVIARY WAS TUCKED AWAY behind the rink, a small nondescript building with a sign including a golden eagle sitting on top of a pile of broken hockey sticks, each one emblazoned with the logos of our rivals. The owner, Liam Canton, was a really good guy, supported the Eagles with a fiery passion, and cut us all really good deals on some fine coffee. It used to be a place where I could find some quiet, but now it was another obstacle I had to overcome.

Part of me hoped that Jacob had given up and gone back to his house.

I pushed open the door, the warmth rushing out, and quickly shut it behind me. Nothing had changed in The Aviary. After what had happened before Christmas, I felt as if the seismic shift in my own life should've been evident in everything else, but the tables were in the same places, and the coffee bean poster art hadn't moved. The scent of coffee was still mouthwatering, the cakes under glass remaining a temptation I couldn't pay for right now. The place was empty, all apart from the tall man at the back.

"Scott." Jacob stood from a table and gestured me over. I took off my coat and left it on the hook and then headed toward him. Normally we'd all sit at the window, but maybe this table was one way of not letting anyone see that Jacob was meeting with me.

Did that make Jacob my only friend?

He fist-bumped me, then looked past me to the front of the shop. Before we could exchange hellos, the door swung open, and the cold blast of air reached us, even in the back, and I saw Ryker and Ben.

I wanted to run. Shove my way past them and just get away.

You're a coward. Luke wouldn't be pussyfooting around like this. Tell them you're sorry. Then fuck off out of their lives. You don't need anyone.

My dad's voice in my head wasn't a new thing. I was quite happy to judge myself by my father's standards after everything I'd done. I knew I wasn't Luke, not strong like my brother or brave or confident. Even with people I knew well, I was wondering what I was going to do next. Ryker turned back to the door, locked it, and turned the sign to *closed*.

"You don't have to lock the door. I'm not going anywhere." The inevitability of getting punched was strong, but I'd face it like a man. Or fake being strong. I was good at that.

Ben immediately stalked over to me, anger on his expressive face. "This is an intervention, and you're not leaving until we're done," he snapped.

Ryker huffed. "Jeez, Ben, it's not an intervention, dude. Scott's already getting help."

Ben shoved at Ryker, who stood his ground and rolled his eyes. Then Ben turned back to me, and there was palpable tension in and around him.

"It's a friendship intervention," he stated, and I winced. This didn't sound so good, and I wanted to get in first.

"I'm sorry," I blurted. "For losing my shit and hurting

you." I checked briefly for the damage I'd done to his face, but other than a faint mark above his brow, there wasn't much to show, certainly not an ugly scar. He didn't acknowledge what I'd said, and that hurt badly. All I needed was for him to say he was okay with it and then to tell me to fuck off. At least then I'd know where I stood.

"You know what *they* told me?" Ben said, and I hadn't been expecting the switch in the conversation. Did he mean Jacob and Ryker?

"Who?" I stood my ground, despite the fact that Ben took a step closer to me. I'd already decided I'd let him pummel me a bit, just to get his own back, but my instincts were clearly having second thoughts as I stiffened.

"They," he repeated. "All the people who don't know you as I do. Dad told me to stay away from you, and Mom agreed. She said I should give you time, let you settle down, that I shouldn't rush things, and I listened because I'm a good son, and I respect my parents. Then, when I couldn't stay away any longer, I went to your place, and your dad said you didn't want to see me. Told me it was all the team's fault. So I accepted that at first, okay, because fuck you, I feel guilty I didn't see what was happening. *I should have seen.* I went back to your place, and your dad gave me this huge speech about fault and reasons and how I supposedly was your best friend and how I should have seen you."

"No, Ben—"

"Shut up, Scott," Ben snapped. "Then, you see, I spoke to a counselor informally, and he said I should let you have Christmas because once you were back with family, then the last thing you needed was me up in your face, reminding you of how we all failed you. I shouldn't text you; they all said that. My parents, your dad, the counselor. All I knew was that maybe you were in withdrawal or rehab or fuck knows what. Not that I knew a damn thing." He poked me hard in the chest. "Because you never told me. I stayed away, but I'm done with all that psycho mumbo jumbo. You're my best friend, and I don't want to hear your apologies. I want to get back to how it was between us, but fuck it, I also want to work out where it went wrong."

I was as stunned by that speech as I had been when Hayne had likened me to a white knight, and I didn't know what to say to Ben either.

"We need to get back to normal," Jacob emphasized and stood next to Ben, his arms crossed over his chest. What exactly *was* normal? "How do we achieve that? What can we do to help?"

Ryker moved as well, the three of them forming a wall between me and the door.

Jacob elbowed Ryker. "We'll help you fix things," Ryker said immediately, and I saw this for what it was, a choreographed speech that they had planned between them, which made me feel a hundred emotions all at once. I was overwhelmed with fear and love and all those little reminders of pain.

The three of them were part of the problem, even if they'd never meant to be. Ben with his perfect fucking family, and Jacob with his solid focus on the future. Not to mention Ryker with his charmed life and people who cared. All I had was Dad. It wasn't as if Mom was present enough to care, lost in grief herself. I wasn't the same as my three friends. I was broken, and it hurt so bad.

"I want to be your best friend, Ben," I murmured.

"Jacob, I want things to be normal, and Ryker, you can't fix everything. I just need time."

Ben clapped a hand on my shoulder. "It's been four years since Luke died, Scott. I know you had your black moments, but I really thought that you'd somehow—"

"You thought what?" I interrupted tiredly. "You thought I'd come to terms with him dying? Or found a way to get past what happened? I wish it were that easy."

Particularly when it was me who argued Luke should go on the spring break trip. Me who persuaded Mom and Dad, back when they actually loved me.

Ben shook his head. "I didn't think any of that, but maybe I hoped for things. It's just you never talked about Luke, and I thought for a long time that you'd decided to bury it." He pulled back his shoulders and mirrored my pose. "It was easier to believe that than to actually be a friend."

My heart hurt, and I reached up to place a hand over his. "And it was easier for me to let you all believe I was okay."

"So what *can* we do now?" Jacob asked. Jacob was all about having solutions for problems.

What did I do now? Did I tell them I wasn't living at home? That my dad had lied to Ben? Everything was spinning in my head, and I felt nauseous. I desperately wanted to get back to Hayne's loft, just to sit on the mattress and watch him paint, maybe even get a handle on my emotions. What I'd felt last night on that blow-up bed was peace and quiet from the monsters inside my head and the people outside who I couldn't talk to. In the grief group, Monica had talked briefly about carving time out to listen to yourself, about being selfish and making space to think. I hadn't been listening to it all. In fact I'd been staring at the splashes of scarlet on Hayne's jeans at the time. But some of it must have sunk in. There was peace in Hayne's place. There was acceptance and no questions, and I knew I needed that for the next few days at least, so I decided to be honest and direct.

"Thank you, all of you." I held out a hand to Ben, and he gripped it. "Ben, I'll never stop being your best friend, but all I want to do right now is apologize, and I can't get my head around everything, so can I just get some more time?"

Ben stared at me, then gave a nod. "I want us to get a coffee, tomorrow, here, same time, even if you bring a book and just sit there. Can you do that?" He appeared uncertain as if he felt I was going to tell him no. Sitting, with a coffee and a book, and just knowing Ben didn't hate me was something promising.

"Yeah," I said.

We didn't stay long, splitting up, Ryker muttering something about how he'd never seen me read a book, and me cuffing him around the back of the head.

It wasn't back to normal, but it was a quiet step in the right direction.

I just wanted to go back to Hayne.

What was it about Hayne that had me so twisted in knots? Was it grieving me who was clinging to his support and friendship? Was I confusing his caring for something else? I caught him peeking at me this morning, his smile soft, his eyes warm as if he was seeing me and liking what he saw. For the first time in months I felt a flare of something back, for him. A poke of attraction that had been a small flame at first but was slowly becoming something more. I loved the way he moved, the way he lost himself in art, I loved his smile, and I wanted to kiss him.

I'd never wanted to kiss anyone as much as this.

How could I even think of kissing, and more, when my head was still so fucked up?

Because Hayne makes you think that all things are possible.

It had only been just last night, but there was a definite attraction, and it was becoming my happy place—an all-consuming desire that outweighed all the other crap in my head.

My cell rang as I was crossing the quad, kicking at the snow piling up on the edges, and all thoughts of kissing Hayne vanished when I saw it was my mom calling.

"Mom?" I answered and stopped dead in the middle of the path.

"Scott, darling, how was your Christmas?"

I pulled the phone away from my ear and looked at it in disbelief. This was some kind of twisted joke, right? My mom finally deigned to contact me, and that was her first question? How about asking me where I was staying, or if I was eating okay, or hell, anything but what my freaking Christmas was like.

I heard her calling, the tinny voice small as I stood in the snow. Slowly, I put the cell back to my ear.

"Sorry?" I asked because maybe I'd just heard wrong.

"We missed you at Christmas," she said. And there it was again, a complete disassociation from real life. Same as every other day in Mom's life. She'd never been present for me or Luke, but since his death, she'd found solace in drink and solitude, shut away in her room. I'd tried to be Luke for her for the longest time until I realized she didn't see the world the same as other people.

Grief is a funny thing, an all-consuming hate, a fear that grips a person, a whole mess of lies you'd tell yourself to get through the day. I knew how she felt, and all thoughts of kissing Hayne, of actually feeling something golden in among all the gray, vanished.

"I wasn't invited," I managed to say, and I heard her tut, as if I'd gotten it all wrong that Dad had said he didn't want to see me ever again.

"Your dad…" she began to say something which might have turned out as something profound, but of course it never went anywhere, same as always. I needed a strong mom. I was desperate for some glimmer of the love I'm sure she had for me, somewhere. "Anyway, never mind. I have to go. I have a facial booked."

What?

"Okay, Mom," I said, and then the call disconnected, leaving only silence.

That was the weirdest conversation, but I wasn't surprised by any of it. By the time I made it back to Hayne's place, I'd rationalized it all. Mom was losing her shit, Dad was a bastard, my brother was dead, and that just left me.

There was a note from Hayne saying that he would be late. I loved that he even thought I needed to know his movements, loved that he cared enough to let me know.

Am I just filling the void with him? Is he what I need? How much can I hurt him?

I curled up on my blow-up bed, determined to wallow in my grief, only something about this room, the scent of paint, the memories of Hayne's smile, and the quiet way he connected with me refused to allow in the darkness.

So I picked up the nearest book, an introduction to biochemistry, and was soon lost in research.

And all the while, I kept an ear out for Hayne coming home.

SIX

Hayne

"HAYNE, TELL ME AGAIN WHAT THE INSPIRATION FOR THIS work was."

I stood beside Professor Poole, my idol, and the only reason I had come to Owatonna U instead of the Rhode Island School of Design. He was a petite black man with a pronounced limp and an inner eye that had created some of the most alluring expressionist art I had ever seen. His work had hung in The Tate, the Pompidou, and the Guggenheim. *The Guggenheim.* I *dreamed* of seeing one of my paintings displayed in the Guggenheim.

"Uhm," I mumbled, then spit out the curl I had been mouthing. "That snowstorm two weeks ago."

He assessed me from over the top of his skinny half-moon glasses. I began chewing on my hair again.

"Surely there was more to this work than snow." He moved around my winter knight painting, his old, weathered cane tapping on the classroom floor with each step. "I've not seen this kind of passion in your work for quite some time."

I spit out the curl, wishing now that I hadn't hauled my painting to the art department for him to grade. I should have left it in the attic. Kept it as mine, holding it close so that when Scott left, I'd have a remembrance of the man who had moved not only into my space but had also taken up residence in my heart. The crush I had on my attic-mate was monumental. And sure to end in heartbreak.

"It was a powerful storm," I told my professor. He gave me another look of disbelief, then paused at the right-hand side of the canvas.

"It's an exceptional allover painting. The attention you gave to ensure that the entire composition reaches all four corners and that the paint and color swirls to the edges of the canvas is delightful. And here"—he lifted his cane to point at the winter knight in the center of the storm—"this bleeding of the colors speaks of a wise hand holding the brush. Too much pewter would have given the form a darkness that would have made the knight of the storm too present. The blending is superb, although there are some places around the shoulders of this ethereal being that I think would have been better suited to a fan brush or your fingertip."

I nodded.

Professor Poole lowered his cane and leaned on it. "I'd like to present this to the Minnesota Museum of American Art's executive director to see if she'd be willing to hang it in the upcoming 'Winter's Wrath' exhibition."

"Huh?" The curl fell out of my mouth. Professor Poole chuckled. "But I…"

"It's by far the best piece of work to come out of this student body in twenty years and is your most inspirational and passionate painting. It's a lusty, stirring oil that screams masculinity and vibrates with nature's rage. With your permission, I'll call Diana and have her drop by the campus to see it."

"Oh, yes, please, yes. Thank you, Professor!" I grabbed at his fingers resting atop his cane to shake one, or both. Instead of yanking them free and making him teeter over, I squeezed his rough, dry hands tightly. "I'd be honored. Thrilled. Will she like it? Do you think? Should I take it back home and try to blend—?"

"Hayne, stop and breathe." He gave me a warm smile. I started breathing again. "I'm sure she'll be as taken with it as I am. I'll call you after I speak to Diana. Go on home and locate that muse of yours. Whatever or whoever it is, you need to keep it close at hand."

I ran to the door, bounced off the frame, turned beet red, and then raced out of the small art and design building. Speeding around the English building, I crashed into a big guy in an Eagles varsity jacket hustling along, head down, fliers tucked under his arm.

"Whoa, you okay?" he inquired as he steadied me. He had curls kind of like mine, thick but not as kinky. He was really pretty and had a nice smile, but that didn't stop my initial fearful reaction to the big guy.

"I'm good, yeah, sorry. Oh, your fliers!" Several had escaped during the collision, and the winter wind was blowing them across the quad. We ran after them, grabbing them from bushes and snow-covered benches, one swirling upward in a whirlwind of snow, then gently floating to earth to land by our feet. I bent down and picked it up. "Sorry, here's the last one."

"It's cool. Keep it," he said as I held it out to him. "Maybe you and your girl can attend. It's a booster event for the hockey team. Trying to raise money for a new Zamboni."

"I know someone who plays on the team or did," I said as I read over the leaflet. A Valentine's dance at The Aviary sounded kind of fun. I never went to campus events. No one ever asked me, and if I did venture out alone, it always ended badly. Better to stay inside with my paints and my music. Less deep-sixing went on that way.

"Yeah, who's that?"

"Scott Caldwell." I folded the pink paper and shoved it into my backpack.

"Really? You wouldn't be Hayne, would you?" I blinked up him. "We've been meeting for coffee between classes. I'm Ryker Madsen. He talks about you steadily. Says you're an artist and that you took him in. Thank you for that." Ryker then hugged me so hard my spine popped a few times.

"Uh, yeah, sure, he's…" I waved a gloved hand in the general direction of home. "There're things at home I have to do."

Ryker gave me a randy wink. "Yeah, I have farming things at home that I really want to do too." He nudged me with his arm. I stumbled off the path into a snowbank. "Oh, sorry dude."

I smiled and began walking in reverse to get some distance between me and the big sporty guy. Even if he did seem nice, jocks can turn on a person like a demented Doberman.

"If you see Scott, tell him I said to bring those notes I let him borrow tomorrow!"

"I will," I said, waved, and then raced home, throwing glances over my shoulder from time to time in case Ryker decided to come after me. One didn't look like, act like, or weigh as little as me and not be paranoid in this world of toxic masculinity.

When I hit the foyer at home, I stripped off my winter gear, and up the stairs I went, eager to find Scott and tell him about the painting. I rounded the corner on the second floor and nearly went to my ass as my sock-covered feet slid across the worn carpeting. Craig stepped out of his bedroom, grabbed me by the arm, and pushed me into the wall. The back of my head bounced off the thin wallboard. When I tried to tug free, he tightened his grip on my upper arm until I winced.

"Listen up, freak, this shit of that hockey player living here and not coughing up cash for the rent is at an end."

"He's looking... ouch, would you let go?" He squeezed harder. I hated Craig with a burning passion. The feeling was mutual, obviously. "He's looking for a job. As soon as he gets one..."

"He either coughs up a hundred bucks for rent, or he gets the fuck out. And don't think that because he's a jock, I'm not going to kick his ass out the door. I play baseball, Dexter plays football, we both have issues with him living here rent free, and we both have the muscle to haul him out of your bed, you freakish little queer."

"Hey, you know the lease is in my name, right?" I snapped.

He showed me a fist. "You know *this* is in *my* name, right?"

With that, he flung me to the side. I fell over the first step leading to the attic, my hair obscuring my sight. I sped up the stairs and exploded through the door, my heart pounding and my legs quaking. Scott was spread out on the air mattress, using the old tongue-and-groove wall as a backrest. He glanced up from his textbook, smiled just for a moment, and then let the smile slip.

"You okay?"

I slammed the door shut. "Yes, fine. Good. I… ran all the way from campus," I panted, then bent over to take off my socks, whipping them into the hamper by the small fridge.

"Why?" He closed his book, and all his attention rested on me. I felt funny inside, fidgety and fluffy, airy, hot, needy, confused and—"Why did you run?"

"Oh, I have news. Good news." I threw the door a look, then hurried over to sit on the air mattress with Scott. He had super long legs, thick and hard from skating, but I made sure I curled into myself on the corner of his bed so not to touch or crowd him. "Professor Poole really likes the *Winter Knight* and is going to call the director of the Minnesota Museum of American Art to see if she'd like to add it to an exhibition they're running now. Or was it a new exhibition? Shit, I can't remember, but if she likes it, one of my paintings might be in a museum. And people will walk by and see it! Some will pause and study it and make soft thoughtful sounds as they enjoy the color scheme and brush strokes!"

Scott laughed softly. "Man, you are super stoked. I'm really happy for you." He grabbed my toes and squeezed them. I giggled, then hid my face in the floppy neck of my turtleneck sweater.

"You were the knight," I whispered into the soft wool.

"So you keep telling me." He patted the top of my foot,

and then his sight flickered from mine to my feet. "Dude, really. You have paint between your toes. When did you paint last? Like, four days ago?"

My ears and face turned scarlet. "Stop, I do not." I slapped at his hand, but he pulled my leg out and up to show me my toes. Shit, there *was* paint between my toes. Sunshine yellow, to be exact. From the new oil on the easel that I'd started one morning when we'd woken and seen that the snow had melted off the skylights. The sun had fallen on Scott, and well... I had had to paint.

"You so do." He chuckled. I tugged on my foot. He playfully held on to it. "I've never seen such tiny toes. They're like little macaroni."

"Don't make fun of me!" I snapped, the giggling and roughhousing coming to a quick stop.

"Hayne, hey, I'm not." I tried to kick him in the face for saying I had macaroni toes. "I'm not making fun. I think they're... beautiful."

Face hot with shame, I stopped trying to drive my heel into his handsome face. Bracing myself on arms locked behind me, I sat there, stunned, as he lifted my foot to his mouth and pressed a tender kiss to my little toe.

"Your feet are small and delicate, the arch high, the skin soft and pale and dotted with paint." He spoke and kissed each toe, and then came a light touch of his lips to the sole of my foot. My cock was hard as a post. I had never experienced anything so erotic. Scott caressed my arch, his gaze roaming over me, touching on the erection tenting my leggings, and then slowly coming up over my heaving chest to my face. "Would you be... can I... is it okay if I kiss you?"

"Yes, please, if you would," I squeaked as he placed

my heel on his lap and leaned up, his hand cupping my chin. I closed my eyes and puckered. He blew several wild curls out of the way, then put his lips on mine. The kiss lasted for a second or two, the pressure so light I barely felt it, yet I felt it all over. He pulled back and let his fingers slide along my jaw.

"That was nice." I opened my eyes. His were fiery. "Your lips are as soft as the skin on the sole of your foot, which you did *not* wash in the shower."

"I did wash my foot. I just missed that spot," I replied in a weak, raspy voice. "I'm happy to have you here to talk art with."

"You happy about my kisses too?"

"Yes, very much."

His smile lit up my attic in ways the sun wished it could. He pulled me into his arms, wrapping me tightly in his embrace, and fell back to his air mattress, wiggling us around until he was the big spoon and I was the little spoon. I'd never been happier to be flatware in my life.

"Tell me more about your amazing painting," he whispered beside my ear.

We talked for hours, lying like two tablespoons in a warm, soft drawer. I fell asleep in his arms and didn't stir until my phone alarm went off.

"Pretzel knots," Scott grumbled. I snorted softly, slipped out of his strong arms, and crawled across the floor to find my phone. "What is that?"

"Mendelssohn's *violin concerto in E minor, opus 64*," I prattled off as I silenced the cell phone and sat down in the middle of the floor, hair covering my face, a yawn cracking my jaw. "I need to call Mimi and Mom about the picture."

Scott mumbled something, then left his air mattress. I slid around on my ass to watch him walk to the small corner bathroom. He'd started getting lax on the whole privacy thing over the past couple of days. I sat there, arms around my legs, fixated on him taking a leak. His upper half was bare, his bottom half in worn flannel sleep pants.

"Should I not call them or call them? If I call and *Winter Knight* isn't chosen, then they'll be upset."

"Then don't call them," he called over his shoulder.

I wrinkled my nose in thought. "What if they find out I knew and didn't call them? What if they found out you know but not them?"

Scott flushed and turned to look at me. "Then call them."

I nodded. "No, I don't think I should."

His eye roll was epic. "Flip a coin," he said, spinning from me and dropping his sleep pants to the floor. My eyes flared at the display of tight ass. Then he was gone, behind the white curtain. I pushed at the morning wood in my dusky blue leggings. The water came on, the pipes rattling and moaning in the wall. I turned on some music to drown out the groaning pipes, then snuck around the room, taking off my clothes from yesterday and gathering up clean clothes to wear to class.

"What's this?" Scott shouted from the shower stall.

"Still Mendelssohn, just a different opus," I yelled back just as the water was shut off. I did my best to tidy up as he dried, to give him some privacy. I was pulling some milk and day-old Danish from the fridge when he threw the curtain aside, the rattle of the rings pulling my attention from breakfast.

He'd pulled on jeans and an OU sweatshirt in the

Eagles colors of gold and brown. His hair was finger-combed, his cheeks thick with dark scruff. He looked me up and down. I blushed as his sight lingered on my skinny chest.

"What the hell happened to your arm?"

He stalked over to me standing there with a half-gallon of milk and a cold, dry, raspberry Danish, and I instinctively skittered into reverse, my ass bouncing off the fridge. I held the milk in front of me like a shield.

Brilliant, Hayne. Plastic will protect you. Try lobbing a stale Danish at the next slob who shoves you around.

"Hayne, it's cool." He lifted a hand and tugged gently on a kinky strand of hair fluttering back and forth in front of my mouth. "I will never hurt you, right? You know that?"

"Yes, I know. I'm just…"

"What is this?" He released the curl and poked at my biceps. I hissed in pain, then glanced down at the purple ring around my upper arm.

"Ugh, stupid Craig."

"Craig? Like that douchebag roommate of yours? *That* Craig? Did he do this to you?"

I shrugged, trying to play it off because I could sense the anger starting to bubble inside Scott.

"He was just horsing around, you know, grabbed me too hard. I'm delicate as you said," I lied, hoping to avoid any kind of confrontation. "Hey, I forgot!" I slid my elbow from his hand and jogged over to my backpack. "I ran into your friend Ryker on the way out of Willows Hall."

"Yeah?"

"Yep, he was nice." I grabbed the pink flyer from amid

the books and papers crammed into my bag. "He was hanging these up. Some sort of Valentine's Day booster event for the hockey team. Local band, food, dancing. No booze, since this is a dry campus."

I handed him the flyer. He read it over quickly. "Did you want to go or something?"

"I thought... well, if you were feeling up to it, then maybe we could check it out." I peeked through my hair. He seemed really tense. Perhaps it was the bruising, or maybe it was the thought of going out and being seen with me. "Unless you don't want to go with me, which I totally get. You could go by yourself and be with your friends. Isolating ourselves isn't good for our recovery. We need to be with other people and... what?"

He shook his head and murmured about not fitting in anymore.

"That's not true. They're all your friends," I told him as his sight locked onto the flyer, which I was beginning to wish I'd never brought home.

"That party's for the team. I'm not on the team anymore," he stated, lifting pained eyes to me. "I don't deserve to be there."

My mind raced to find something to say that wouldn't sound trite or patronizing. I opted to go with the truth. He'd be able to see the sincerity in my eyes.

"You'll *always* be a member of the team." He frowned and muttered. I could hear the paper in his hand crinkling. "It's true. Are you saying that injured members of the team are no longer considered Eagles hockey players?"

"That's different. That's a physical injury."

"And you're fighting back from an emotional injury.

Hey, no, I'm serious here. When I lost Jay-Jay, one of the first things my counseling taught me was that a person must heal physically *and* mentally from any trauma. We all try to push past the mental health aspect of things, but you can't, you know?" He stared right at me, right into my soul, his gaze seeking something that I hoped he would find. "Addictive and destructive behavior is a symptom, just like pain in your leg when you tear something. So you're recovering from a deeply bruised psyche, and that will take time, just like a bad knee. Real friends all know this and will never turn from you."

A long moment ticked past. I worried I had pushed him too hard, had been too greedy and pushy, too whiny and clingy. Too desperate...

"You're an incredibly giving person."

My cheeks grew warm under the praise. "Do you want to try it, then? The party? You can go by yourself, if you'd rather."

"Why would you think I'd go to this stupid thing without you?" he asked, folding his arms over his chest.

I blew hair out of my face. "Because most people don't want to do things out in public with me."

"Fuck that. Okay, here's the deal. From now on you do not put yourself down in front of me, okay?" I nodded. He cocked an eyebrow. "Seriously, I mean it. Hayne, you are beautiful and magical and so full of kindness and love. You make me feel... I don't know how I feel, but I like it. Please, don't repeat what losers like Craig and Dexter have pounded into your head. You're special, and I would be proud to go to this Valentine's Day thing with you."

"Really? Like, touching and stuff in public?"

"Exactly like touching and stuff in public."

There were no words, so I whispered a weak thanks and scurried to the bathroom and yanked the curtain around me. Then I hugged myself tightly and did a small, silent happy dance.

SEVEN

Scott

THE GROUP WAS QUIET TONIGHT. WE'D ALL ARRIVED, helped ourselves to coffee and the donuts that Monica had brought with her. I sat in what I thought of as my usual chair if I had one of those having only attended two sessions so far. Hayne sat opposite me now I didn't know if that was because he felt comfortable there or that he wanted space or because he didn't want the rest of the group to know we were...

What? What were we to each other? Hell, if I knew. Apart from friends, of course. He hadn't asked me to leave his place, and I'd stayed fourteen nights now, and we talked as if we were friends. But there was more; a spark that I couldn't ignore, a gentleness Hayne had in him that I was drawn to, and of course that had ended up with the one kiss we'd shared.

We hadn't done anything else since, apart from cuddling. Maybe that was what I needed, just to be able to be close to someone who knew some of the grief and pain that consumed me at times. I didn't question what we were doing because it felt right. Anyway, whatever the reason, I could've sat and watched him paint for ages and just as easily hugged him for longer.

He raised an eyebrow at me, and I sent him a wry smile as I realized I was staring. He'd changed before we'd come out tonight, today's jeans covered in splashes of orange and red, or copper as he pointed out. I saw the individual colors; he just saw the beauty of them together.

I'd already proved I wasn't an artist when he'd offered me a brush and I'd made a halfhearted attempt at painting a square. That had been this morning, and he'd carefully taken the brush from me, explaining that not everyone had the ability to paint.

He'd only taken the words back when I'd pinned him and tickled him. Which had turned into cuddles and talking softly about the color red and squares and all kinds of artistic things that meant so much to him.

I wanted to kiss him again. I could weigh all the pros and cons, come up with conclusions to support a kiss, and equally enough issues that meant I should really leave him to get on with his life.

I was a selfish bastard. I felt safe in Hayne's place, and I wanted to stay.

"Has anyone seen Alice?" Monica asked, then checked her watch again. This was only the third session I'd attended, but Alice had been there each time, picking at the fabric of her cardigan and saying things when prompted. Last session, she'd gotten into an argument with Oscar over the use of the word guilt. Monica had wanted to know if any of us felt guilt that we'd lived when our loved ones had died, and that was like a red rag to a bull, apparently.

The things I could have said at that point about how if

it hadn't been for me, Luke wouldn't even have gone on spring break. What would anyone say to me if I explained that guilt consumed me, and it wasn't because I'd lived; it was because Luke dying was all on me. So I'd stayed quiet, but Alice had snapped something I didn't really hear, and for some reason, she and Oscar ended up in a heated debate. They'd hugged it out, and everything had settled, but her absence tonight was clearly worrying Monica.

"She told me she was coming," Oscar said from his position by the window. He was staring down at the entrance and probably willing Alice to appear, pulling out his phone and texting. To her, I assume. I caught Hayne's gaze, and he looked worried. Should I be worried as well? What weren't people telling me here? Were they thinking something had happened to her?

"Should we call 911?" I blurted.

"What for?" Alice said from the door when she breezed in as if we hadn't all been just sitting for five minutes wondering where she was. She was bright-eyed, smiling. There was a spring in her step, but no one could miss the stumble as she walked, and I could smell alcohol as she sat. Seemed to me as though she was self-medicating, which is what I'd been doing for a long time. Like knew like.

She patted my knee, then blew a kiss at Oscar, and Monica closed the door to the room to begin the session.

"Alice, there's coffee," she prompted, but Alice shook her head.

"Don't want to ruin my beer buzz." She laughed and slumped in her chair, leaning into me. "Alcohol is good." She breathed up at me, and the fumes hit me square on.

There was a silence for a moment. Then Monica cleared her throat. I knew she wasn't there to judge, but she certainly appeared concerned. "Welcome everyone, tonight I thought we would talk about…"

The rest of her words were blurred. All I could focus on was the scent of beer and how liquor could blot out everything. What would everyone here think of me if they knew just how much shit I'd done when I'd been drunk? I doubted anyone here was the type who to attend frat parties, but the shame that washed over me had to be making me scarlet.

You think alcohol is going to help? You think it will bring back Luke? Dad's words snapped at me, dredged up from yet another nasty scene when I'd done nothing to defend myself.

What if Hayne found out some of the things I'd done? There was a connection between us, a nebulous but shiny thing that made me feel warm. If I told him what I'd done under the influence of drink, he'd turn and run. I remembered throwing my weight around, I recalled the shit I'd said to people. Then there was a lot of stuff I didn't remember at all. People expected me to be a jock, the kind that messed up people and thought they owned the world, and I'd played that part really well. As each memory piled on top of each other, I'd worked myself up into such a state of shame that when it came to my turn to talk, I didn't even know where in the process we were and what I was supposed to be saying. Alice snored softly and drooled on my shoulder, and I didn't dare move in case she fell, but all I really wanted to do was go and find a beer. I couldn't play hockey, I didn't need to gain muscle, I didn't need to care about myself, and alcohol sounded good right about now.

Hayne looked right at me, biting his lower lip, an errant curl falling over one eye, and his posture still. He'd be so disappointed at the things I'd done.

"Scott?" Monica pressed.

The itch of needing to leave was beginning to steal my rational thoughts, and I moved a little to test if Alice would fall. As a result, she slumped against me. *I can't move.* I felt trapped, closed in, and even though I knew I should breathe through this panicking shit, my brain instead defaulted to temper.

"I wasn't listening," I snapped, wanting to lash out and hurt.

Monica ignored my rudeness. "Oscar was telling us about his dad and what he meant to him." She hesitated, obviously searching for some reaction from me.

"What? How can anyone…? Wait, you really want me to talk about what my dead brother, my only brother, meant to me?" I asked, horrified at the thought of telling anyone the details of what kind of brother Luke had been. "I can't…"

Alice mumbled something as I shifted to get comfortable. Then she cursed, and before I could get out of the way, she sat bolt upright, vomited on the floor, narrowly missing me, and then curled up and began to cry. I didn't know what to do. I should've comforted her, but it seemed everyone wanted to help, and I stepped back, frozen with what I needed to do and only just holding on to my emotions. The session ended then, but I still didn't move, not until Hayne took my hand and led me from the room. We were halfway home, fighting our way through the bitter wind before it hit me what had just happened. Abruptly the nebulous thoughts in my mind coalesced into clarity, and I stopped walking.

"What's wrong?" Hayne asked.

"I drank a lot," I blurted and attempted to pull my hand free of his. But he wouldn't let go, and I was irritable with being trapped, yanking hard and releasing his hold, shoving my hands into my coat pockets so he couldn't touch me again. "Just like Alice, I would be permanently drunk, and my hockey suffered and my studies, and they were telling me my play was sloppy so that was why I looked to the steroids as a solution. At least I think so. Or maybe I just wanted desperately to fuck myself over, hit rock bottom. I don't know."

Oh God, where was this all coming from? I'd never said this to another soul, not even the high-priced counselor my dad had gotten for me when my drinking had become obvious. Funny how he'd wanted to help with that, but the steroids had been a step too far.

I thought he'd wanted a hockey player for a son. I needed those damn steroids.

"We all have our issues," Hayne said and moved closer to the tree we'd stopped under, probably to get some shelter. "I once ate my entire body weight in chocolate and was sick for days."

I knew he was trying to lighten the tone, but there was no comparison in overeating chocolate to what I'd done, even though I didn't say a word. How could he think his grief was anything like mine? He needed to back off and leave me alone because I was done with him if he thought losing a friend was as bad as being responsible for your brother's death. I wanted to punch something, make a fist, and make myself bleed. Pain banded my head, and I felt dizzy.

Then he cradled my face with his gloved hands and held me still.

"Breathe, Scott," he instructed, and for a moment I struggled with the order, but then something in the way he looked right into my eyes and the emotion in his words shoved aside the temper and righteous indignation that had flooded me. Rational thought began to return, and through all of it, I kept breathing. Finally, I was done, the testosterone-fueled temper subsiding until all that was left was the hollow grief that was my constant companion.

"Scott? Are you okay? Should I call your friends? I don't have anyone's number."

Jesus, the last thing I needed was them to see my meltdown, which was far too similar to what had happened in my last game. That time I'd hurt Ben, and this time I could have hurt Hayne.

"Shit," I said with feeling, and he went up on tiptoes and pressed a kiss to my lips.

"Thought that might help." Under the old tree, in the swirling snow and ice, I wanted to pull him close and kiss him like there was no tomorrow.

I didn't. I wasn't ready for that yet, and it wouldn't be fair on Hayne. I was broken and not ready to kiss a man I liked. Nowhere near ready.

"You know, I don't have numbers for your friends. I should have them."

"Okay."

"I could meet them someday." He sounded so hopeful, but I wasn't ready to share him yet.

"One day, yeah."

Brief disappointment marked his expression, but it cleared when he smiled softly. "You don't need to share with me, yet. Come on, let's go home," Hayne said after a moment's pause, then began to walk away.

"Hayne," I said urgently, and he turned back to face me. "I would understand if you wanted me to find my own place. Ben said he could put a mattress on his floor…"

At first, Hayne seemed sad, then confused, and then he smiled. "Please stay," he murmured then shrugged. "It feels right."

"SO BEN IS the starting goalie? Is that the right term?" Hayne asked me, leaning forward in his seat and staring down at the ice. We were here for the Eagles/Bowling Green Falcons game, and we weren't that far from the team. I could see them talking to each other. I'd even caught a couple of them staring up at me, but I hadn't held their gaze. Did they resent me? Did they hate the fact that I'd fucked up and now had the audacity to actually come to one of their games?

Ryker sketched a wave after Ben nudged him, Jacob nodded in acknowledgment, but others weren't as forthcoming. Add in people sitting with us who made pointed comments about cheating and lying, and then the housemate, Craig, sitting two rows back and staring daggers at us. I didn't know what his problem with Hayne was, and wished I'd remember more about this party the other housemate said he'd met me at. Unfortunately, it was another event blotted out by alcohol. Maybe I'd tried to prove that hockey players were harder than Falcon guys. Maybe I'd kissed him?

I glanced back to see his sour expression and instinctively knew he wasn't the kind of guy I would have tried to kiss.

Why the hell did I think this was a good idea?

Oh yeah, because Hayne had guilted me into it, and I couldn't resist the brown eyes that brimmed with emotion as he'd told me he'd *never* understood hockey, and how he'd *never* been to a whole game, and how it would make him *really happy* if I could do this for him. I didn't say yes after all of that, but when he straightened the blanket on my mattress and side-eyed me, he knew he had me. After all, he had given me a bed for nearly three weeks. We'd slipped into domestic harmony, making each other drinks, taking breakfast in turn, and I'd given him whatever tips I'd made from each shift at the pizza parlor. It was a small amount against what I could give him when I was paid properly, but he wasn't happy about taking the tips at all. He had a brightly colored rainbow jar in his closet and he put all the tips in there, saving them for a rainy day, or so he said.

We didn't have to pay for tickets today. Ben had seen to that, saying he was intrigued that I was bringing my artist friend with me to a game.

"He's too arty to like hockey," Ben had said, then frowned at me when I punched him in the arm. I'd lectured him on not judging books by covers and explained how much of a good guy Hayne was, and added that I thought Ben was an asshole. All of which made him flustered and me as well when he commented how passionate I was. Then we'd tussled, and I'd been triumphant for all of ten-seconds when he'd rolled me and sat on my belly. For a moment we'd been old Ben/Scott, and it felt good.

"Earth to Scott," Hayne repeated and poked me in the side. "Ben is in the net tonight, right?"

"Sorry, yeah, he's a wall. Just watch."

"And your other friend, Ryker, he's the one doing that stretchy thing there?" He pointed at Ryker and then leaned against me. I eased away. I didn't want Hayne to become a target for any shit tonight and certainly didn't want the cheating-lying thing to morph into an anti-LGBT *thing*.

"Yep, jersey with Madsen across the back, and Benson is Jacob. He's a defenseman, keeps people away from Ben."

"Do you wish you were down there?" Hayne asked, then sipped his soda.

Did I wish that? Did I miss hockey? Hockey had been my entire life, even before Luke died. I'd wanted to be just like my big brother, wanting the NHL scouts to come and watch me, wanting to win games like Luke did with fancy moves. I'd hero-worshipped him, and I'd shown some talent. Not enough to make it to the NHL as Luke would have done, or as Ryker had, but surely enough to get me playing somewhere at a lower level. That was my accepted future, and for the longest time I'd thought that was what I wanted.

Until I began to mess up, until I wasn't good enough, until I'd begun to ruin things for myself, just to show Dad I was my own man. Then the drinking started, then the steroids, *and now* look at me.

I'm truly lost.

"Yeah, I miss it," I answered finally. I wasn't really lying, because I did miss the camaraderie and the feel of my skates cutting into the ice. But I didn't miss the pressure at all. Dad had never let me rest, assumed things for me, demanded I try harder, to be *better*.

He didn't acknowledge I had a skill in chemistry and numbers, that I could do other things with my life away from hockey. He only wanted a replacement for Luke, and I'd been too stupid to argue or show him what else I could do.

"It's starting," Hayne shouted over the chants and clapping. He had a wide grin on his face, and it made me smile back. Maybe if I saw hockey through his eyes, I could find the love I'd lost for the game. It was worth a try.

The Eagles won the first face-off cleanly, the puck shuttling between Ryker and John as smoothly as if I was still there. We'd been good together, the three of us. Ryker on wing, me on the other wing, and John as center. We'd been a formidable line that defensemen on opposing teams found hard to counter, but down there now Cole was in my place, and I couldn't help feeling that everything was wrong.

EIGHT

Hayne

HOCKEY. WOW.

I'd never experienced such a raw, passionate sport in my life. Of course, I'd never experienced any sport because, well, I was Hayne Ritter, that freaky, skinny art guy who always got picked last for any team. Unless you counted Pictionary as a sport...

Hockey was all speed and bone-crunching hits, blood and guts, vibrant hot colors, auras of red and orange, aggressive tones. And Scott had been a part of this stormy, wonderful, masculine game. Sitting beside him as the teams went at each other made me long for him in ways that mere roomies shouldn't long for each other. I wanted him to love me in that blind, hot, sloppy, rough carnal way that men loved one another in all the porn I'd watched. Since I had no practical knowledge of hot, sloppy man sex because... well, just because I was what I was, I had to assume sex was gritty and loud and really slippery.

"Oh! Oh! Did you see that thing that Ben did?" I shouted at Scott when the Eagles goalie did this big, arcing kicking-his-skate-in-the-air move to block a puck. "He's a god! A war god! You all are war gods! Battling other gods, the earth trembling and shaking as the titans skate on ice of blood red and batter each other with flaming sticks!"

Scott smiled at me.

"I have to paint," I said breathlessly.

He blinked in surprise. "Now? I mean, we only have ten minutes left of the game and—"

"Now, right now. The colors are here." I poked myself in the forehead. "The imagery. I have to paint." I grabbed my scarf, tied it around my neck, and began crawling over spectators, the rush of creativity coursing through me.

"Hayne! Oh, for fuck's sake. Sorry, sorry, oops. Sorry, ma'am. Hayne!" I heard Scott coming along behind me. He grabbed the end of my scarf and tugged me to a quick stop. I spun to face him. "Do you have to do this *now?*" He looked at me and then back at the ice. Oh, he wanted to stay.

"Yes, right now. I'm going to wither if I don't. But stay. Watch the game. Please. I want you to be with your fellow warrior gods." I tugged my scarf from his fingers, rose to my toes to kiss his whiskery cheek, and then ran out of the rink, the urge to paint growing hotter and hotter.

When I hit the foyer of my house, I was so winded I thought I might pass out. I didn't though. I tore off my coat and kicked off my boots and left them lying by the front door. The TV was on in the living room, something with loud explosions. Not caring what my other roommate was doing, I barreled up the stairs to my attic. As soon as I stepped inside and inhaled the aromas of paint and turpentine, my muse took over. She, and yes, my muse was a she and her name was Persephone, gave the canvases along the far wall a studious glance and whispered to me that we needed a wall canvas, for the battles of the gods could not be contained on anything smaller.

"Yep, right, so right." I pulled a massive canvas out from behind standard-sized ones. I made my own when needed, and this one had been sitting for ages, waiting for the right moment and the right work. "This is the right work," I said, kicking aside shoes and empty soda cans to clear space. The canvas sailed to the floor, scrips and scraps of paper billowing outward when it landed. I peeled off my socks and whipped them at our beds. Wound in the rapture of a new painting, I grabbed a few tubes of paint. One aquamarine, one ochre, and one Venetian red, to reflect the various colors of battle and armor I'd been witness to. A mental image of Scott geared up and knocking other warrior gods aside formed in my mind, and I whimpered with the beauty and need it created in me. It scared me half to death to be so enamored of a man I knew so little about, but he was stunning, and my artistic eye wanted nothing more than to feast on him indefinitely.

I tapped the play button on my paint-speckled stereo, and my messy studio was filled with Puccini. Wearing just my jeans and an old sweater, I stepped onto the wall-sized canvas I'd stretched over a handmade frame. It was a big one, measuring ninety by seventy inches. The canvas sagged in the middle. I'd reframe it when I was done, but for now, the muse was whispering in my ear, and I had art to create. Making wall art was like waltzing with the colors. I loved the feel of the paint on my hands and feet. It opened me up to the process as a whole so much better than a paintbrush could. I grabbed the tubes of paint from my palette table and gave myself up to Persephone and the music.

Vissi d'Arte faded into *Liebestraum* by Liszt. I tossed the cap from the ochre to the corner and squeezed the tube. Then I did the same with the aquamarine and the red. Eyes closed, the music leading me in the dance between art and artist, I dropped to my knees and pressed my hands into the cool paint. Blindly, I pushed to the left, and then in a circle, hearing the colors as clearly as I could hear Liszt. The rush of creation swept over me, pumping me full of passion and chaotic need, I slid forward on my knees, fingers slippery with paint, and ran my hands to the end of the canvas. The hair on my arms rose. Chopin's *Aeolian Harp* began to play. I opened my eyes, and Scott stood in the doorway of my studio, his smile uneven, his beautiful eyes glowing.

"Beethoven led me here."

"Chopin," I corrected instantly, then chided myself for being a snob.

"Right, Chopin. We won."

"Awesome!" I sat back on my paint-coated heels.

"Is this the battle of the gods painting coming to life?"

I nodded. Curls fell into my face. I blew them out of the way.

"You must have been really into this one. I picked up your coat and boots and took your keys out of the front door."

He tossed the keys onto the shelving unit that held my supplies, then walked to the canvas. His right shoulder dropped just a bit when he walked, so he tended to swagger. It was masculine and confident and everything I wasn't. "So is this some of that Impressionable art that they taught us about in high school art class?"

"Impressionism." He rolled his eyes. I bit down on the inside of my lower lip. *Stop correcting the big people, Hayne. It makes you sound elitist,* "No, it's not. Impressionism is known for its brush strokes and open composition. Most are outdoors, and... you're bored."

"Not at all. So what is this then? Finger painting for grown-ups?" He gave me that off-kilter smile that he threw around like confetti on New Year's Eve. It never quite made it all the way to his haunted eyes though or rarely did. I wished his eyes could be happy all the time.

"Sort of," I confessed. "It's maybe some sort of experimental art." I shrugged. "I like to do them when I'm feeling... hot and inspired."

"You're always hot, Hayne. It's one of the things I like about you." He sat, pulled off his socks and OU hoodie, and then stood and made a move to join me.

"The canvas won't hold us both," I warned him, but Scott, it seemed, didn't listen well. He stepped onto the tightly stretched canvas, and the staples began to fly. One hit the brick wall and then ricocheted off the window pane.

"Duck and dive!" he yelled, throwing his arms over his head and falling to his stomach on the canvas. I shouted at him to stop, but he rolled to his back, his chest and face smeared with vibrant, angry colors. He smiled up at me, a sincere smile, that made his eyes glow like a warm gemstone. "Hit the deck, Picasso!"

He grabbed me by the arm and jerked me down, looming over me to pin my back to the canvas. I slapped at him, knowing moving someone as beefy as he was would be impossible. He snickered madly, sat on my stomach, and rubbed his hands over my cheeks.

"Stop! Oh come on, do you know how hard this is to wash out of hair like mine? Blech! Argh, it's terrible!" I tried to grab his wrists, but he was too fast, too strong, and too hell-bent on pushing as much paint into my hair as he could. "Dammit, Scott!" I snarled, which only made him laugh a little harder. Chopin's *Nocturne* began to play.

"You're cute when you're mad. I've never seen you so lively."

"You're a big, pushy jock." I planted my hand on his pectoral, then jerked it away, leaving a red handprint on his skin. He glanced down and nodded in approval. "Get off me."

"You sure you want me to do that?"

"What?" I asked, my voice mousy now that the ire had leeched out of me.

"You sure you want me to get off you?"

"Scott... I..."

He fell forward, catching himself on his hands, his nose now a mere inch from mine. I couldn't breathe right. My skin felt hot with static, the fine hairs on my arms rising. I peered up at him, into him, trying to see if this was yet another time when the athlete was jerking the dweeby art guy around, but I didn't see pity or disdain in his gaze. I saw desire and something else, respect or admiration maybe? There was a small droplet of red by his eye. I had to touch it and work it into his skin. How I ever found the courage to caress him so intimately I don't know, but I touched his face, using that drop to make a curlicue.

"Curlicue for you, Boo," I muttered because I'm a flaming asshole. I lay there under him, eyes wide, chest tight with mortification, heart slamming into my breastbone.

"You're too fucking cute," he whispered, then covered my mouth with his.

I gasped at the first contact of his lips on mine. They were so soft, so perfectly formed, and then they were demanding. My eyes drifted shut, and I opened for him, letting him lick into my mouth while Strauss filled the room with a glorious waltz. Scott lapped at the corners of my lips, making me chase his tongue with mine. He was delicious, hot and skilled. He nipped at my lower lip before coming back to my open mouth to taste and tease. I needed more. He ground his hips against mine as if he knew that was what had to come next. The music exploded over us, shaking the skylights with sheer volume. He mumbled something. I agreed to what it was he'd said. Then his hand slid into my pants, his fingers brushing over, then wrapping around my cock. I cried out. Scott and the music captured my yelp of pleasure.

"You want this? You want me to get you off?" he asked, his words hot on my swollen lips.

"Yes. Do it. Get me off." I sounded so sure of myself, so gruff, so unlike me. "Please." Ah there was the Hayne we all knew so well. "Please yes, I want you…"

"I know you do," he purred, stroking me from base to tip, twisting his palm over the wet head of my cock. "I want you too. Come for me, Hayne."

He buried his face in my neck and worked me hard and fast. I came with a shout that only I heard. Scott used my spunk to ease the friction. I dug at the canvas under us, my hips jerking with each shudder of release. Scott mumbled my name, then let go of my dick. Grabbing a hip to hold me in place, he rocked his cock into my leg, over and over until his big body shook.

"Hold still, shit, yes," he huffed beside my ear. I didn't move a muscle. I couldn't have, even if I'd wanted to, which I didn't. I was too spellbound listening and feeling his orgasm rock him. "God, ah God, that was fucking amazing."

He lifted his head to gaze at me. I felt my heart skip several beats. He was so beautifully powerful and so painfully weak, a wild and chaotic blend of things in one gorgeous man, who had blown into my life like a winter storm. Only Scott hadn't given me any warnings. There was no red sky or fluttering weather flags the day we had met. Which was probably for the best because a man like me would have hidden from the signs of an incoming typhoon of angst and lust like Scott Caldwell.

"Your curlicue isn't curly anymore," I announced and then painted a new one on his chin, which he found to be stupidly amusing. That spurred him to paint one on me and then kiss me again, this time with a softness that surprised and captivated me.

He rolled off me, the canvas frame creaking as he flopped onto his back. "I think we should name this masterpiece, *Semen and Storms*," he said, then slapped the canvas hard. Another staple popped off and hit the wall with a metallic little *ping* that made us both laugh. "What do you think of that name? Bet they won't have another one like that in the art gallery."

"What makes you think anything of mine will ever be in an art gallery?"

I'd still not heard about *Winter Knight* being hung in the museum...

He pushed up to an elbow, then reached over to flick some sticky hair from my cheek. "Because you're a fucking genius, Hayne Ritter. Just look at how nicely you've painted me."

"You're the most beautiful canvas I've ever worked on." *Wow, could we be any lamer, Hayne?* "I mean, you're the most beautiful man who I've ever had sex with. And I would love to paint you again... I mean, not literally like this, but... I loved the hand job." *Yep, we can be.*

That broke him up. He pulled at me until I was splayed over his chest. "I don't remember the last time I laughed like this with a guy. Or anyone. You're a beautiful canvas too, Hayne."

Heat crept up my neck. I liked him saying those kinds of things to me. I liked the way he touched me and kissed me, and I *really* liked the way he made me feel as if I belonged with a man like him.

We lay there until the paint on our skin began to harden. He went off to shower, leaving colorful footprints on the hardwood floors. I decided to leave them there because soon he'd be stronger, and he'd leave this dingy little attic with the virginal artist behind. When he was gone, I'd have those prints to remind me of this amazing night when we had created something glorious and passionate in shades of fire and desire.

I slithered off the canvas, my skin coated with drying paint and my hair a knotted mass of curls, sodden with orange and vermillion paint. The front of my underwear was damp with cold cum. I was a horrid mess, yet I felt like a newly formed star high in the heavens. I got to my feet and studied the painting lying on the floor. The colors had been well mixed—that was for sure. A tiny blush colored my cheeks. I glanced from the canvas to the corner where Scott was washing. I wished I could see him under the water, his skin slick and wet, his cock hanging spent and limp along the inside of his thigh. My dick kicked. Then the door to my attic blew open.

I spun around and nearly went on my ass. The floor was nothing but paint splatters and colorful footprints.

"I swear to God, Ritter, how many times have I told you about this freaking asshole music of yours?" Craig thundered into my space and threw a look around the attic. "I'm trying to cram for a test, and you two queers are up here screaming and playing this stupid shit music. I pay rent! I deserve some quiet!" He stalked to the stereo, his bulging eyes and fisted hands spelling out his intent pretty clearly.

"No!" I shouted, sliding over to the stereo and placing myself in front of it. "I'll turn it down, I promise. I'll never play it loud again."

"Get the fuck out of the way," Craig snarled, then shoved me into my palette table, the paints and brushes falling to the floor as the table rocked up and fell over. I went to my ass.

"No! That's my Mimi's! No, don't hurt it!" I yelled and watched in horror as Craig reached for the old stereo. Then Scott was there, in nothing but clean underwear and wet hair. I shimmied in reverse, crab-walking over the canvas until my shoulders met the wall.

Scott was truly a warrior god. Fury roiled out of him as he slammed Craig against the wall not once or twice but three times. The two big men pushed and shoved. I curled into a ball, my chin on my knees, my arms tight around my legs, and watched as Scott easily maneuvered Craig out of the room, shutting the door after him.

I could stil hear Craig shouting. Thuds and curses seeped around the doorframe. A moment passed, maybe two, and I couldn't stop shaking. Then Scott opened the door. He scanned the room, his chest working like a bellows, his gaze rife with ferocity the likes of which I had never seen in those hazel depths before.

"He won't ever use that word in front of you again," Scott said, his voice thick and gravelly.

"Did you hit him?" I inquired, but the words were weak and mousy, so I asked again. "Did you hit him?"

"Yes." He padded over to me, dropping down into a crouch as I processed. "Hayne, no one treats you like you're nothing *ever* again." He lifted a crusty curl from my nose and tucked it behind my ear. "No one ever says hateful things to you ever again."

I wet my lips. "Thank you for saving me. You really are my winter knight."

"Go shower. I'll clean up." He kissed me on the lips so sweetly that I uncurled from my protective ball and wrapped myself around him. Somehow, he managed to stand with me hanging off him like a lemur. He carried me to the shower, peeled me off, and then left me to scrub myself. I stayed under the water until it ran clear, shampooing my hair several times to get it clean. With a towel around my waist, I peeked around the curtain to find that Scott had cleaned everything up, even his bright red footprints. That made me sad. What would I have of him now when he left? The massive canvas had been propped up in the corner. Scott was in his bed, watching me with wary eyes. His chest had paint on it again from when he'd carried me to the shower.

"If you want me to go tomorrow, I'll go," he said, the stereo sitting still and quiet. I stared at him in confusion. "You probably don't like guys like me, ones who use their fists to solve disputes, and I get that. So if you tell me to go, I'll go."

I crossed the room and knelt beside him on the air mattress. "Come to bed with me."

"I... wait, what?"

"Come to my bed. Stay in it, please."

"But that outburst with Craig..."

"Yeah, that was pretty damn awesome." I stole a kiss. "Will you sleep in my bed with me?"

He replied by sweeping me into his arms, then pushing to his feet. I squealed and giggled as he carried me to my bed, then laid me on it reverently, as if I were a fine china dish or a delicate crystal statue.

"Are you sure about this?" he asked as I wiggled under the covers, then held them up for him.

"As sure as I am that the fire gods are hockey players."

That made him smile, and his smile made me glow. I fell asleep with my head on his chest and my eyes on our fiery, passionate painting, my newfound love for him glowing like an ember in a fire god's kiln.

NINE

Scott
___

I COULDN'T BELIEVE I'D LOST CONTROL LIKE THAT. I
couldn't believe I'd punched that dick Craig so hard.

On the ice, when the blood was running hot, it was
inevitable that there'd be pushing and shoving. If a shooter
barreled into my goalie, then you can bet your ass I'd be
all over them, and not just because our goalie is my best
friend, not *just* because it's Ben in net. The team has each
other's backs, as if donning the Eagles jersey immediately
includes a man in a circle of trust. Outside of the rink, I
could usually keep a tight rein on my physical reaction to
shit situations. I didn't shove people who line-jump, I
didn't whale on the idiots who messed around in lectures. I
had restraint.

Except where it came to Hayne, it seemed. When Craig
went at him, I'd channeled everything I'd learned about
how to handle the toxic abuse that Ryker would get thrown
at him. Ryker had told me to hang back, to take a moment,
to meet the abuse head on and challenge it, said he'd

gotten that from Tennant Rowe, and it's all about de-escalation.

De-escalation, my ass. Craig had been all over Hayne, and he was intimidating and horrific, and *oh my God,* the fear in Hayne's expression had torn me to shreds. Then I'd hit Craig. Hard. We were evenly matched for weight and height, but I had two things over him. The fact that I was a hockey player who knew how to use my body to advantage was one. The other was that he was messing with *my* Hayne.

Mine.

Hayne had rolled over in his sleep, and I spooned him from behind, holding him close, protecting him, making sure nothing could hurt him, and I felt like the knight he'd painted me as.

Was that wrong? Was I just as intimidating? Had I crossed a line to come to his rescue? He certainly wasn't some shrinking violet; he was small, yes, but he had a backbone of steel and the heart of a lion. I just wasn't sure he knew it. I thought that maybe in the morning when he woke up, he would want to talk about what happened, and I'd apologize and explain what had been going through my head and how instincts had kicked in.

First of all though, I would tell him that we had to figure things out because right now, I needed him on my team, however selfish that made me. I closed my eyes and tried to sleep, but the heavy weight of guilt over what I'd done began to change and curl and morph into something a lot darker. My chest hurt, my eyes stung, and I extricated myself from Hayne and rolled up and off the bed. My skin prickled and pulled with dried paint, and I stretched until some of the patches separated and I could peel off the vibrant colors. The rest would have to wait until I had a shower, and I wasn't going to do that at four a.m. I was restless, aching, and then as I paced the room, I saw my bag. In there were my skates, and I itched with the need to get on the ice.

I missed the ice, the game, but most of all I missed the camaraderie of the team, some of whom blanked me when I saw them. Ryker, Jacob, and of course, Ben tried to understand me and what I'd done, meeting me for coffee every day so I could talk. Only I mostly sat there and listened to them do all the talking, picking up on the subtle things I was missing out on. The saga of John and his search for the perfect shower gel, the prank on Mitchell that had led to the defender having purple hair, the beers the team had gone out for a few days ago. All of it was happening without me being in the middle of it all.

I ached with the loss. More than I thought was possible, and the rational side of me knew that somehow, I was mixing the grief of Luke's death with heartache at what my family had become and the year ban from the team. It was all there, an infinite vortex of shit that I was slowly being sucked into.

"Scott?" Hayne called from the bed, and I stopped my pacing. The room was gently lit from the lamp we never turned off, and I had never seen anything as beautiful as Hayne sitting in bed, his hair sticking up, his eyes sleepy, his use of my name soft and inviting. "Are you okay?"

"Hey. Go back to sleep." I couldn't stay. I couldn't do it. I felt too big, too stretched in my own skin, too clumsy, and I was the last thing Hayne needed. On impulse, I pulled on jeans and a shirt, and he watched my every move as I bundled up in my coat and picked up my skate bag.

"Where are you going?" he asked.

"Skating." I tossed him his key where it sat on the table. "I'm using my spare key to lock you in. Don't go out and... just don't, okay? Promise me?"

"I won't go anywhere," he murmured and snuggled back down into the covers. "Don't be long."

I escaped as soon as I could, using my key to lock the door. When I went down one flight, I paused and considered waking Craig and laying another warning on him, but what would that do? I'd made my point, and Craig knew I meant what I said.

The door is locked. Hayne promised not to go anywhere.

I hurried then, out into the frigid air, the ice taking my breath as I scurried away from Hayne and headed for the arena. I knew I was early enough to get some skating in because today was an official practice, so none of the team would be anywhere near the place that early. I might have had to share some ice with Lissa the figure skater, but she was a cool chick who would happily move aside and let a guy skate lazy circles. I gripped my stick harder the nearer I got, and only when I was in the locker room did I relax my hold. In jeans and my sweatshirt, I went out to the ice, lacing up my skates without even thinking, waving to Lissa, and then pausing at the gate. The opening was right by the home bench, and I could see the faint marks on the whiteboard that sat on the shelf at the back. The X's and O's meant nothing to other people, but I could see the marks that showed the team had been working on the power play.

I used to be part of the power play. Hell, that was my

biggest strength, backing up Ryker and making space to shoot.

Does the team miss me? Do they see I was someone who gave my all to the team? Or do they see me as a steroid-abusing asshole whose departure might well hurt their championship chances?

There was grief again, the blackness pushing up inside me, and I bowed my head, and I don't know how long I waited there, but I snapped out of it when I heard a yelp.

I glanced out at the ice to see Lissa sprawled right over the center circle, and she wasn't moving. Without thinking, I pushed onto the ice, and in seconds I was at her side, falling to my knees and sliding to a stop.

"Lissa! Fuck," I said and looked around me. *Where was she hurt? Should I call 911? I should. I need to do it now, but my cell is back in the—*

"Will you kiss it better?" Lissa said and snorted a laugh, rising to her skates gracefully and holding out a hand.

"What the hell?"

I stood, without her help, and glowered at her in my most intimidating manner. All she did was grin at me.

"Something needed to happen to get you on the ice, Scotty," she singsonged, then shoved my chest and skated away, executing some crossovers and falling into a sitting spin. I stood absolutely still, watched her through narrowed eyes, and then she skated so close I felt the rush of air. "You need to move, moron," she teased.

So I did.

I didn't think I would ever forget how to skate; I'd been a skater since I was three, when that was all tumbling to the ice and laughing like a loon as my big brother swept by me. I remembered Dad dishing out drills. Not to me, I was too little, but Luke was always being given a list of things to do. *Work those crossovers, get your balance. What the hell do you call that? Jesus, Luke, your little brother could do better than that. Stay on your damn skates, kid.*

Me? I was stepping around the ice having the time of my life as my dad shouted at Luke, and Mom sat with her book not really watching us at all.

It was funny how certain images could stick with you. Like finding Luke crying at age eight, when I was only five, him telling me that his ankles hurt. Or discovering him in our shared bathroom when he turned sixteen, crying because he'd had his heart broken. Or that moment I'd waved him off on spring break, seeing him smile, grateful because I'd fixed it with Dad for him to go. I'd been the one to talk Dad around. I'd made Dad see that Luke needed time with friends when I'd explained to him that all work and no play made Luke pissed and it showed in his playing.

Giving Dad what he wanted to hear had been a particular strength of mine, but why Dad had listened to me that bright, shining day, I'll never know, because he let Luke go. Positively encouraged him out of the door with a promise he'd come back a more focused hockey player.

Luke had never come home.

The grief hit me like a sledgehammer, and I came to an abrupt halt just by the Zamboni door, gripping the wood, staring down at my glove, and dropping my stick to the ice.

He never came home.

"Scott? Hey, you dropped your stick." Lissa buzzed

around me like a fly, nudging me, tugging me away from the wall, skating backward, guiding me in that lazy circle I'd been trying to do. She skated over to my stick and dropped it over the wall, then came back to me. "Lift me," she ordered imperiously, and I released her hold and held out my hands encased in the hockey gloves.

"How exactly," I said, worried she was coming on to me, concerned that I'd done something to give her the idea I wanted to pick her up.

"Take them off, then stand absolutely still." She left me then, circling me, as I took off my gloves and tossed them with the stick. Then she held out her arms. "Brace yourself. Balance with me." She leaped at me, scaring the hell out of me, but I caught her close, and she wrapped her legs around me and let go of her hold. Abruptly I had a handful of arched figure skater.

"Shit, Lissa, I'm going to drop you."

She twisted in my hold. "Lift me higher," she demanded. I didn't have a choice. She weighed nothing, and in seconds I had her over my head. She laughed as she arched her back, then swung herself down to finish the move with a pirouette and a smile. "Now let's skate."

I really didn't want to argue with her, and together we did a circuit of the rink.

"Now faster," she said and set off, turning to face me, and then just as quickly jumping to skate hard. She did a whole lap while I thought about it, and then I was with her. I matched her speed in the corners, but on the straights, she had everything going for her, and she sped away. We skated like that for what seemed like hours, and by the time we stopped, I was sweaty, and my mind was blank, and I felt like I'd done something real for the first time since the crap that had me thrown from the team.

She left then, and it was only six thirty, so I skated slow circles and welcomed the burn in my muscles. I sensed someone else joining me, but I didn't see them until a body stopped me skating and a very familiar figure grinned at me. Ben.

"Scott, let's work."

"Ben, I—"

"I'm having issues with my glove hand." Ben took up residence in the net, looking every inch the goalie, bouncing on his skates, waiting. "Come on, do me a solid."

I retrieved my gloves and stick, not sure how I could say no without appearing like a complete asshole and took the bucket of pucks Ben had, and scattered them on the ice.

What if I've forgotten how to do this?

I corralled the first puck, the weight of it against my stick reassuring, then, blades cutting into the ice, I sent it toward Ben. It was a nothing shot, direct, easy to stop, and Ben stretched out after catching it and sliding it back.

"Again," he ordered.

We did this all the time, spending hours on the ice, me shooting pucks at him, both of us learning from each other. Correction, we *used* to do this all the time. I hadn't been on ice with him in weeks, but something clicked inside, and abruptly I was back with accuracy and strength. It took up until puck eleven, but finally I got one past Ben's glove, and I did it again and then again, and each time he whooped, and I threw a celly, and there it was... I was back.

Of course, when he skated off the ice, chattering on

about some game he was playing with Ryker online, I realized I wasn't back at all. It was just a few moments of normalcy, nothing more.

Ben left first, only because I hung back. The last thing I wanted to do was spend time discussing what we'd just done, and me staying back meant that Coach Quinton found me, cornered me, and gave me the look.

The look that said, Scott, you are fucked.

"Scott," he began. I edged away slowly, heading for the door. "I have a proposition for you."

I stopped trying to escape and waited for him to explain.

"We're looking for someone to work with the kids on a Tuesday and Thursday, short drills, some team building, the ten and eleven-year-olds. Not much in the way of money, but they could benefit from some help from you."

I couldn't help the snort of derision. "Yeah, right, like the parents are going to want me anywhere near their kids."

Coach settled that glower on me. "I vouched for you," he snapped. "You want to make me look stupid to the hockey moms?"

"No, Coach," I replied instinctively, my hockey player heart falling right in line with the coach.

"I'll email you the schedule, be there on time for your first session. Don't be late."

"Yes, Coach."

"And I want you and Ben to set up regular practice. You want back on the team next year, you work your ass off to keep up your skills."

Did I want to be back on the team? Probably not if it meant dealing with my dad and the pressure of academia with sports and the fact that my world view had shifted. I'd need to talk it over with Hayne. He made me see my life in a very different way; not the blue-white of ice but through a prism of rainbow colors.

"Yes, Coach."

He grunted something. "You keeping okay?" he asked, staring at me as if he could see through me.

"Yes, Coach."

"You want to talk about anything, I'm here. In fact, I want to see you in my office each week before the Thursday kids-shift."

I could've said no; I wasn't on the team, he wasn't really my coach anymore, but I didn't say any of that.

I nodded. "Yes, Coach."

As I walked back to Hayne, I felt lighter, or if not lighter, then at least not weighed down with blackness. I stopped just outside the door, left hand pushed into my pockets, my gear over my shoulder, my stick gripped tightly, and stared at the number on the wall. The digits gave me a focus, and the anticipation grew for talking to Hayne, telling him about Lissa with the lift, and Ben with the glove side issue, and teaching kids skills, and having to talk to Coach.

The door opened before I could open it myself, and Craig came out, his eye turning purple.

"Fuck, if it isn't the ice-skating fanny bandit," he sneered.

"Fuck, if it isn't the lawn fairy meathead," I shot back.

"Fuck you, asshole," he said and pushed past me.

"Not with all the lube in the world," I muttered, and he shot me a look that spoke volumes. Still, he didn't stay, rushing away and nearly falling onto his ass on the ice.

When I went upstairs, the door was still locked, and when I went inside, Hayne lay on his back staring at the sky through the skylight.

"Okay?" he asked, and the single word held so many questions that I am sure he wanted to ask.

"Are we?" I began and realized immediately I was being far too cryptic. "I mean, are we okay? Did I fuck it all up?"

He sat up and shook his head. "No, I promise you didn't."

I sat next to him, making sure to leave my sweaty gear by the door. We knocked elbows, and I couldn't help but feel lighter when he took my hand in his and linked our fingers.

"You know what, Hayne? I like it here."

TEN

Hayne

WINTER STAYED AROUND A LONG TIME IN MINNESOTA. I was kind of glad of that because if it was cold and ugly outside, Scott tended to spend more time inside with me. We were... well, we were something unique and special. We kissed and laughed a lot, jerked each other off even more, and slept wound around each other. He was my first lover and my first love. I'd come to realize how much I loved him two days ago when we'd been going through the stack of textbooks in the corner that we could trade at the campus bookstore for money. It wasn't any kind of huge thing; no angels sang or such. I just looked up from book sorting when he'd tugged on a curl. He did that frequently and for no apparent reason. Our eyes met, and my pulse skipped several beats, and I knew he now held my heart.

So yes, the books would bring us some cash. Not much money, for sure, but some. We were two perfect examples of poor college students. I brought home the old baked goods every Friday when I locked up Cream the Beano for the weekend. Nothing like staying alive with stale doughnuts and ramen noodles. I was happy, though. Super happy. Happier than I had ever thought I would be.

Backpack stuffed with old books, I stumbled into the campus bookstore and nearly wiped out a rack filled with OU bookmarks and highlighters.

"Sorry, sorry," I said to the rack as I righted it.

"No worries, it's always getting knocked over." I glanced around the rack to find Ryker, Scott's friend, smiling down at me. Ah, no wonder the rack stood back up so easily. He was on the other side helping. "Guess I need to find a place away from the front door to set it up."

"Yeah, hey," I said, hiking the hundred pounds—or so it felt—of books up over my shoulder. "Hi, Ryker."

"Hi, Hayne." He jerked his chin at the huge bag on my back. "Trading some in, eh?"

"Oh, yeah, the attic is really full what with my art stuff and Scott's hockey stuff. Plus, we need the money."

"Let's see what you have here." He lifted the backpack off me, and I sighed in relief. "You know it's not going to be close to what you paid for them, right?"

"Yeah, I know." I followed him to the counter, glad to have that weight gone.

"How are things at Cream the Beano?"

"Meh, it's dull during classes, but between classes I sell a ton of coffee." I blew some curls out of my face and helped Ryker stack all the books into a neat pile.

"Okay, this will take a bit. I have to look up the books online and see what we're giving on trade-in." He lifted the top textbook and looked at it as if it were some weird alien artifact. "*Art History and the Restoration of the Sistine Chapel*. Sounds… riveting."

I giggled a bit. "It actually kind of was. It's an artist thing."

"Hey, it's got to be better than some of the books my boyfriend reads. Graphic pictures too, like of palpating cows." My eyes flared. "Yeah, dating a farmer is a life experience."

"You two seem happy though," I said off-handedly while I played with the edge of a book dealing with nineteenth-century art.

"We are." His smile nearly blinded me. "I can say the same about Scott, too. During our coffee breaks, he's always talking about you. He's totally wrapped up in you."

I could feel my cheeks glowing. "I'm not sure about that," I mumbled, flicking the edge of the book with my fingernail. He'd never said he loved me. Of course I had never said it to him either. Maybe he didn't love me as I loved him.

"Trust me, the dude is crazy about you. Hey, you're coming to the party tonight, right? The Valentine's one for the hockey team?"

"Oh, I don't know. Scott hasn't said anything about it…"

"Ugh, what a shithead. I'll text him and remind him."

"No! No, don't do that. If he wants me to go with him, he has to ask me. That's how knights behave."

"Knights?" His dark brows were tangled.

"I mean… knights like uhm, I have to get to class." I waved at the mound of books. "Can you total those up and give Scott the cash? Thanks. Bye!"

I ran for the door, colliding into it when two girls pushed it open. They laughed. I muttered an apology, then ran outside.

As I padded across campus, I began to really notice all the hearts in all the windows and all the couples walking along holding hands. I wanted that too. With Scott.

All during my Art 403 class, which was two hours long, I mulled over how to get Scott to ask me to that dance/party thing without appearing desperate. When Professor Tritchie, who was also my department advisor, tapped me on the back of the head with a paintbrush, then pointed out that my canvas held nothing but a blue dot, I made up some sort of crap about it being a conceptual approach to the infinite number of pixels that comprise a drop of rain. She looked at me over the top of her paint-speckled glasses.

"Uh-huh. Well, since this is going to be your senior independent work and must, in some way, correlate with your senior thesis, I suggest that you may wish to add a few more dots or read up on the cellular structure of raindrops. I'm rather sure they're not comprised of pixels."

"Yes, Professor."

Ugh. Class couldn't end quickly enough.

Pixelated raindrops. Brilliant, Hayne. Focus on school and not Scott. You've got a thesis to write and a senior independent work to start. Stop daydreaming about a stupid party on Valentine's Day with a man who will move out as soon as he's able.

I really hated my inner me at times. Not as much as I hated that blue dot, though. I swiped a brush through it, glowered at the indigo smudge, and then asked for a new canvas. The new one sat there untouched until class was over. Then I ambled home, careful to tiptoe up to the attic in case Craig was prowling the house. He did that now, prowled and threw dark looks whenever he saw me. I seriously considered asking him to leave, but I was afraid to do so. Life really sucked when you were a Hayne.

"Hey, where were you?" Scott asked when I slipped inside the attic. It was nice and warm up there, and the air smelled of Scott's aftershave, and turpentine. It was an erotic smell to me. "Ryker handed me a fistful of money over coffee. We're rich!" I tugged off my socks and joined him on the bed, sitting cross-legged in front of him. "Between your old books and mine, we've got over eighty bucks."

I frowned at the four twenties and five ones lying on the crocheted covering. I'd known that the trade-in would be meager, but shit, that was really horrible. I guess art books weren't high on the resell listings or something.

"Forty-two dollars each." I sighed.

He cupped my chin and lifted my eyes to his. "Okay, what's wrong? I mean, I know it's not a fortune, but it's over forty bucks. We can buy some real food with it or maybe go to a movie."

"I want to go to the Valentine's Day party tonight!" I blurted out. His blue-green eyes widened at the explosion. "I do. I know you don't because of things, but I want to go and dance with you and hold your hand and have people know that you're my Valentine, even though we never really said we were Valentines, and we're not really serious or exclusive—I'm exclusive of course because no one wants to date a mop-headed queer artist—but all the doors had hearts on them, and I've never been to a party with a man I care about, and I... this is nothing about the blue dot and my senior thesis... okay, it kind of is because Professor rapped me on the head during class for daydreaming about you and me doing a waltz at the party when I should have been painting, but I don't know how I got here to the blue dot, but I think it's kind of confusing you, isn't it?"

"Uhm, no, not really, yes. Yes, I got seriously confused there." He kissed me before I could spout more stupidity. My eyes drifted shut as soon as his soft lips touched mine. I chased him for more kissing when he leaned back and broke the kiss. "I didn't think you did jock parties or wanted to hang with athletes."

"I want to be out with you. Just once before I graduate I want to go to a college event with a man who desires me."

"Then we'll go."

"Yeah?"

"Yep, but you have to open this letter that came for you today." He pulled a long, white envelope out from under his ass. "It's from the Minnesota Museum of American Art."

"No," I gasped, my heart now lodged in my throat. Scott grinned at me and tapped the return address on the envelope. "No, oh no. I... do you think they want it? I thought they'd call or text or email or... no, oh no." I buried my face in my hands. "Open it for me. No! Don't open it."

"Why not?" He tugged on my hand. I shook my head, curls sliding back and forth over my splayed fingers.

"No, I can't. If they turn me down, it will ruin our Valentine's Day night out. Let it sit until we come back."

"Are you sure?"

"No..."

Scott chuckled, kissed my finger, and tore open the

envelope. "From the desk of Diana Ford-Gray, executive director and blah blah blah…"

"I'm going to faint," I said into my palms.

"I'll read faster," Scott said. Then the room fell silent aside from my heated breaths against my hands. "Uhm… excellent showing of vibrant imagery, color, and bold dramatic contrasts. Wonderful saturation, symmetry, and depth. Uhm… something about organic shapes of winter and nature, flowing forms and focal points. They would be thrilled to include *Winter Knight* in the Winter's Wrath showing. Please sign and return the enclosed permission forms, and we will include your work in the exhibition beginning March 1 and ending April 1. Thank you… look forward to working with you in the future… promising career ahead… blah, blah, signed Diana Ford-Gray."

"Oh. My. God." I fell into his arms, crying into my palms. Scott scooped me up and held me close, rubbing my back, kissing my curls, and showering me with congratulations and praise. I wiggled around on his lap, took his face between my hands, and kissed him hard and long. "You're a blessing, Scott. Without you, this would have never happened! My love for you is all over my work! Oh! I have to call Mimi and Mom. They have to come see it in the museum!"

I leaped off his lap, desperate to find my phone and call home. Scott sat there, letter beside him on the bed, looking at me for the longest time. I bounced around the attic, floated actually, squealing with Mom on the phone, while setting up a trip to campus for them on the opening night of my artwork being displayed. I whirled and danced as I got changed for the party and then tugged Scott up from our bed, red scarves dangling off my neck, and chattered the entire walk to The Aviary.

His smile seemed forced. "We can go back home," I offered to give him one last escape.

"I just…" He glanced at the door, then back at me. "I feel like I'm fronting or something. Like… this is me, but it's not me. It's all weird. I feel like I'm not being Scott, not the real Scott, but I have no clue who the real Scott is."

"Let's go back home," I whispered sadly. He obviously wasn't ready for this.

"No." He straightened his shoulders as if going into battle. "You've done so much for me. The least I can do is take you to a dumbass party."

"Don't date me out of pity," I snapped back, then blinked at my harshness.

He turned to face me, took my face in his cold, cold hands, and kissed me with such passion I felt light-headed.

"I'm proud to have you as my date. Let's do this."

I felt bouncy as we entered, my fingers biting into Scott's arm as the music engulfed us. It wasn't Brahms or Strauss that swallowed up our words; it was JAY-Z or Gucci Mane or some other popular rapper. We no sooner were inside than his friends swarmed around us. Massive, hulking guys crowded in to clap Scott on the back, shake his hand, or ruffle his hair. I clung to him tightly, smiling nervously when he introduced me as his date. Ryker and his boyfriend Jacob where there, as well as Ben, the handsome goalie. Tons of other players and their girlfriends, fans and boosters. People were actually talking to me in a kind manner. No one called me names or taunted me, shoved me into walls or lockers or toilets.

The night was a wild blur of music and eating and

laughter. When they played a slow song, Scott led me to the dance floor—an area where the tables had been pushed to the walls—and took me into his arms in a classical waltzing stance. His hand on my hip, my right hand on his shoulder, my left in his right.

He placed his brow to mine. "I have no idea how to waltz," he confessed as that slow, gorgeous song from *A Star is Born* played. Couples moved around us as red lights, like they have at hockey games, lit up, rotating slowly, throwing scarlet beams over the dancers.

"It's easy," I replied, and oddly enough, *I* led *him*. No one seemed to care if the tiny dude was leading the big dude, least of all Scott. He was smooth and picked up the simple box steps quickly, but his brow remained on my brow, his gaze locked with mine. It was the most wonderfully romantic moment of my life, and I tucked it away in a place where I could examine it later in when it was just me and my paints again.

"Let's go home," Scott whispered after the song wound down. I bounced along at his side, light and airy as a willow-o'-the-wisp, glowing and bound up in my first love affair. We walked back home after saying goodbye to his friends, hand in hand, my mouth running endlessly about the party, his friends, Mimi and Mom coming in three weeks, *Winter Knight*, my thesis, and the puffy little crab cakes at The Aviary, which had tasted nothing like crab.

"I think they were tuna," I said as we stripped off coats and boots and scarves and mittens in my foyer. Well, *I* had scarves, boots, and mittens. Scott usually only wore his varsity jacket. The house was still. Probably Jack and Jerk, aka the Off Brothers, were off with dates. I hoped they stayed gone. I wished I had enough cash not to have roomies. Then it would be me and Scott here, in a big bedroom, and my studio would just be for work and not sleeping, eating, and bathing.

"Did you have the puff pastry?" I asked over my shoulder as we climbed to the attic. "I think they were tuna. I wonder why tuna and not crab? Maybe because tuna is cheaper. I bet so. They were good though," I said, then pushed the door to my room open and glided inside, twirling around a bit, grinning at the flow of my silky red scarves as I did a fine pirouette. Scott stood just inside the door, his aura off. "Are you feeling okay? Did you eat that sushi that John brought? It looked hinky to me. Do you need some Pepto-Bismol or something?"

"Hayne, I think we need to talk."

Oh God, here it comes...

ELEVEN

Scott

_____

Fuck. What the hell did I say that for? Why didn't I word it differently? I couldn't believe how fast Hayne's smile turned to fear.

Fear? Of me?

I stumbled until my back hit the wall, and waited for his fear to ease. After all, if there was distance between us, then he would know I wasn't going to hurt him. Right?

All I wanted to do was explain how I felt, what was going on in my head, but the words that I'd imagined saying had vanished as soon as I saw that fear.

"Just say it," Hayne said. His voice was low, calm, even accepting, like he knew what I was going to say already. How could he know when all the words I had in my head had vanished?

"What?" I asked lamely.

"Say the thing, about the _thing_," he encouraged. "Get it over with so we can carry on with life, or at least so I can."

"What?" Okay, so now I was confused. I thought maybe we were talking about different _things_.

Hayne assumed a stance of not caring. "You're going to say tonight was a mistake, that someone like *me* wasn't the right fit for you, that I'm too..." He waved his hands at the room or at the canvases or the ceiling. Hell, if I knew, but the gesture was tired, not angry. "So honestly I'm okay with it. Just tell me, and we can move on to getting you moved out."

Wait? What? "You want me to leave?" I managed after a pause.

"Of course I want you to leave if you want to leave, and I'm not worried if you go." He crossed his arms over his chest, tilted his chin, and looked every inch a man who didn't care what I did. Only the softness in his eyes and the way his voice wasn't entirely strong and certain led me to think he wasn't really that happy at all.

"I don't want to go," I said, waiting for the sunshine to come back into his expression. That wasn't exactly what happened. Instead the softness I'd seen was replaced by a sudden stony determination.

"Okay, so you're happy to stay. You want to fuck around with me, but you want to keep it behind closed doors. You're embarrassed by me. I get that, but you know what. I've decided I'm worth more than that, and if you want me in here, then you acknowledge me out there."

This was all going horribly wrong. That wasn't what I wanted to say at all, but somewhere in all of this, I'd lost track of everything.

"Dad didn't want Luke to spend spring break with his friends," I blurted out, and Hayne frowned at me.

"What?"

"I could see Luke was tired, you know. He was such a good skater, but Dad pushed him so hard, and Luke was exhausted. All he needed was a weekend away. He had so many decisions to make, about what he wanted from his life. Scouts were watching him. They told him he'd get drafted to the NHL. They promised him a life that Dad could only dream about. My dad nearly made it to the big leagues, or that is what he'll make you believe. He has all these grand stories about how he nearly did this or nearly did that. If you listen to him, he'll make you think he was the next big thing, but that people had it out for him. He was determined that Luke was going to achieve all of this in his place. God, Luke was…" I stopped and slid down the wall until I could draw my knees up and hug them close. I couldn't even look at Hayne, who had gone very quiet.

"Luke was everything I wasn't," I summed up the situation succinctly. "He had this eye for what happened on the ice, and you know what? If he hadn't had Dad hounding him, then maybe one day he could have made it to the big leagues. You know what I mean?" I glanced up, and Hayne nodded, then sat on the floor and crossed his legs.

"Your dad put a lot of pressure on him?"

That was a major understatement. How could I make Hayne see how Dad would push Luke until my brother was bleeding, until every one of his muscles screamed in pain?

"All Luke wanted was two days, that's all, and I told Dad that two days off would make him a better player, that he was tired and just needed to refocus. That was *my* superpower. Dad never expected me to be a player like Luke. He wasn't as hard on me. I just got teased when I fell over. He didn't yell at me, but he made Luke cry the way he focused everything on success. For the first time in his life he listened to me, he said yes, and Luke went with his friends, and he was so happy. I remember his expression. He hugged me and said thank you and that he loved me so much. We didn't do that, you know. We didn't ever say we loved each other, but that day, he told me, and I felt so good."

I couldn't carry on, bowed my head, and scrubbed at my face with one hand. There were still no tears, but the ball of emotion in my throat was choking me.

"That was the weekend that Luke died?" Hayne prompted gently.

"Uh-huh, I just hope that Luke…"

"What, Scott?"

"Nothing." I shook my head. I couldn't give voice to that final fear in my head.

"Tell me."

"I don't want to think of him… suffering."

"I understand."

Of course he did, watching his friend die of cancer had been so hard. Is it better to lose someone suddenly or watch them die slowly? I couldn't imagine Hayne's pain, but I knew that mine was all-consuming.

"I hope it was quiet, that he just sank beneath the water, all kinds of peaceful as you see in films. Just floating to the bottom, without panic. But then, I think, maybe he deliberately let himself go and didn't fight at all."

"You want to be sure that he didn't mean to die?" Hayne finished for me.

Some control inside me snapped. My face was wet, my

eyes stung. I was crying. After all this time, I was actually freaking crying. "Yes," I said.

Hayne moved, came to sit next to me, leaned on my shoulder, and sighed heavily. "Seems to me he loved you so much. Otherwise he wouldn't have said that to you."

"What if it was a goodbye?"

"No, Scott, it sounded like a thank you to me. He was your big brother, and he would have loved you always."

We sat in silence for a little longer, and I laced my fingers with his, letting the silent tears flow and leaning on Hayne for strength. I knew Hayne was right. We had been close Luke and I. He wouldn't have left me deliberately.

It was Hayne who broke the silence, Hayne who gave me the perfect opportunity to make things right.

"So you don't want to leave here, then?"

Hayne wasn't asking me about feelings or the future. He needed me to tell him if I was staying or going, but that wasn't what I meant to say to him tonight. I'd been in this attic space for weeks now, falling for Hayne more and more each day. That is what I wanted to make clear.

"God, no! I mean, as long as it's okay for you, it's just that I don't want to leave the man I'm falling for," I said.

Silence. Not an awkward silence, but enough time for Hayne to think about what his answer was going to be. Fear pooled in my stomach, but at least I had stopped the quiet crying now.

"Well, that's good then, because I think I might already be falling for you, too."

He moved then, crouched in front of me, our fingers still laced. "Let's sleep," he said.

Not fool around or kiss, just sleep. He knew exactly what I needed.

Curled around him, I didn't sleep for a long time, but when I did, I dreamed, and I didn't remember any nightmares chasing me in there.

———

THE FIRST I knew about the video was when Alice slapped me. The entire day had started off well but then grown steadily stranger. I'd met Ben and Jacob for coffee. We'd spent the entire session talking hockey, and I didn't feel the pressure on my chest when we discussed our teams. It was a good start. It was *after* that when things started to get weird.

I heard a whispered "asshole" from behind, turned to see a group of girls staring right at me, and it wasn't because they wanted to look at me at all; it seemed they had an agenda. I offered a small smile, since I get it. I fucked up the Eagles' chances this year, and they were probably hockey fans. When all of them turned their back on me, I wasn't worried. I mean, of course I *was* worried, no one likes to be hated, but I still had the taste of Hayne's kisses on my lips, and I was feeling pretty damn happy.

I got shoved outside my lab class, hard, into a locker, but no one said anything to me, and I chalked it up to being an accident. Then the whispers started and the pointed fingers, and it was halfway through a Forensic Chemistry lecture that my phone vibrated in my pocket. I ignored it. Just like I did when it vibrated again.

And again.

Someone really wanted to talk to me, but I was too focused on the experiment to worry, and by the time I left class, the last out as usual, I'd forgotten the messages. I was meeting Hayne at the grief session tonight. He was coming straight from a meeting about the installation of *Winter Knight*, and when we'd spoken last, he was high on excitement. I was the final one to arrive at the meeting, and my gaze zeroed straight to where Hayne would normally sit, only he wasn't there. At first I wasn't worried. Maybe he was running late. Then my phone started up all over again, and fear gripped me. Had something happened to Hayne? I fumbled with my phone, missed calls from Ben, Jacob, Ryker, and those were just the main ones. Ten missed texts from unknown numbers as well. I opened them up, read three, the early ones, and they were filled with hate.

What?

"Asshole," Alice's hand connected with my face so hard it wrenched my neck, and I stumbled back, hitting the door frame. How could this tiny girl make me stumble so badly? Was she drunk?

"What the—?"

"Get the fuck out of here," she screamed in my face, the stench of alcohol washing over me. She was drunk, her eyes wide, temper slashed across her expression. That explained it all. I needed help here, and it was the moment I looked for Monica that I met Hayne's steady focused gaze.

"Hayne?" I asked, my head still ringing, my face scarlet, and an overwhelming fear that I'd fucked up somewhere along the way.

"We need to all sit down," Monica encouraged, moving between me and Alice. "This is a peaceful session."

Hayne ignored her, took a step toward me, held up his phone, and pressed play.

I didn't get it at first. What was I watching? The motion of the phone was shitty, like the person holding the phone was drunk. It seemed to be footage of a party, and there was chanting, and I recognized Craig. Was this some horrific thing that Craig had done? People did know I had nothing to do with Hayne's housemate, right? Just because we were both involved in sports, it didn't mean we were the same.

Then it changed, and I made sense of the chants. *Scott! Scott! Scott!* The video focused on a man, completely off his head with drink, unable to focus, stumbling, grinning like a fucking idiot, the Scott in the video was holding something, no… someone… by their legs, upside down, and laughing so hard as they did it. I recognized the freshman I was holding, Danny I recalled, a quiet kid, the younger brother of one of the football players, gay, bright, happy. Memories of him saying he'd loved hockey flooded my head with sickening clarity.

"Light as a fucking fairy!" Video-Scott shouted, and there was Craig, slapping me on the back, one jock to another, as Danny fled when I let him go. Video-Scott bro-hugged Craig, a whole chest bump, and the beer he picked up sloshed everywhere.

Craig went up to the phone that was recording this, grinned evilly, and gave a thumbs-up. "One more fucking fairy down," he shouted with glee.

The video ended then, the room silent.

"That wasn't me," I defended.

"It was clearly you," Hayne said, and I realized he'd moved to stand next to me. "You were drunk, right?"

"I didn't mean it. I didn't know what I was doing. I'd taken the tablets… and then I'd drunk so much… I remember the party, but I don't even remember this… Hayne, I don't."

Hayne nodded as if he understood what I was saying, but he didn't touch me or glance at me, simply took his chair for the session. I couldn't breathe. I was sorry, humiliated, shocked, and stepped back out of the room, gripped my phone, and left before I fucked up anything else. I heard Monica call my name, but I didn't stop.

I ran from the building, straight into Jacob, who gripped me.

"I've found him!" he called as I struggled free of Jacob's hold. Then Ryker was there and finally Ben. I closed my eyes.

"What did I do?" I asked no one. "I don't remember."

They took me to the café. I didn't recall how I got there, staring down at my feet, horrified at what I'd seen myself do. I went into the coffee shop first, but they didn't follow me. The place was quiet, dark, but I saw a figure at the table. Danny. The same guy I'd lifted upside down.

"Sit," he murmured, and I scrambled to obey, just because I deserved to do what I was told, and also everything he said to me, every goddamn word of it.

"Fuck, Danny," I managed. "I don't know what I did, why I did it, I swear to you that I'm not like that"

Danny lifted a single eyebrow and gestured to his phone. "Adam wants to kill you," he began conversationally, as if telling me his brother wanted to end my life was just accepted.

"Of course he does."

"It's okay though. I stopped him. He won't hurt you."

Adam was a big guy, but I could defend myself if I needed to against him. Only I had the feeling I would just let him pummel me if he needed to. Just like I'd accepted Ben could do the same to me. I buried my head in my hands and groaned, then forced myself to look Danny in the eye as I apologized. He was different to Hayne, his hair lighter, his eyes blue, but all I could imagine was Hayne sitting opposite me now. I'd hurt Danny and then I'd beaten on Craig to get him to back off of Hayne. What was wrong with me? How could steroids give me such a rage that I'd thought it was okay to hurt another man?

"Danny, I don't know how to say sorry... I'm sorry, so damn sorry. That wasn't me..."

I said the same thing as I'd done to Hayne, *It wasn't me.*

"I know it wasn't you," Danny murmured. I frowned because that wasn't the right answer. He was supposed to say that it *was* me in the video.

"I don't know why I did that."

"Craig spiked your drink."

"I wish that was the easy solution."

"Scott, it is *that* simple. I don't know what he put into your drink, but what I do know is that the two of us went from chatting quietly about hockey and being younger brothers, and then you glazed over, and snapped with so much hate. You were manic, but I put it down to beer and what I call jock-anger."

I hated that he and Hayne even had to have an explanation for the way jocks acted with them.

He pressed ahead. "A few days after the party we were in the lunch queue next to each other, and I didn't see that same hate in your face. You were back to smiling and talking about hockey; it was as if you were two separate people. When the video of what you did hit the net this morning, Craig was gloating about what he'd done. He even came up to me to tell me about it. Thing is, I have friends with phones who caught when he boasted that one pill was all it took to have you hurt me. I mean, does he have shit for brains or what?"

Danny smirked as he said that and tapped his phone. "The video of his gloating is currently uploading, and by this time tomorrow, no one will remember what you did to me, or why, only that Craig is an abusive asshole who spikes people's drinks. I imagine the administration will have something to say to him as well. God knows how many others he's done this to."

"Fuck."

"This will open a whole new can of worms. Are you ready for that?"

I didn't know what I thought. I was lurching from one horrific and stupid mess to another, and in the middle of everything, I was spiraling again.

"Hayne will see what he did," I murmured. "But, Danny, I'm sorry I did that."

"It was the pill he slipped you."

"No, I don't... Is it inside me all the time? Is that what I'm really like? Did I *want* to hurt you? Hayne will see all the ugly inside me and..." I couldn't say anything else, emotion choking me.

Danny reached over and touched my hand. "I wish I could tell you what's inside you, but I can't. Talk to Hayne. He's a good guy, keeping himself safe from a world that doesn't quite understand people like him and me."

The door opened, my three friends entering, Ryker staring at his phone, then fist-pumping success.

"Shared," he said and pocketed his phone. I knew Ryker had a Twitter and Instagram following. Actually, pick any social media app, and Ryker, future NHL star, embraced it.

Hayne would see it wasn't me that had done this awful thing.

Only… what if it was the real me?

TWELVE

Hayne

MY STUDIO HAD NEVER BEEN SO QUIET. NO MUSIC PLAYED, no laughter rang out, no heated huffs of passion lingered on the stuffy air. It was just Scott and me, standing in the middle of our messy space, staring at each other.

"You have to know that what you saw wasn't me," he said again. He'd said that same thing at least five times since I'd unlocked the door to allow him in ten minutes before.

"It looked like you." And that had been my reply to his repeated pleas. I hugged myself hard, avoiding his gaze and focusing on my toes peeking out from the ratty pant legs of a pair of old jeans. "It sounded like you. I've heard that laugh come from you just yesterday. When you laughed at something I said. Were you mocking me then? Were you making fun of me as you were Danny?"

I peeked up.

"No, God, no. Hayne, I just…" He shoved a hand into his hair. I bit down on my bottom lip to make it stop quivering. "Hayne, that's me, yes, but my drink was spiked."

I shook my head, curls curtaining my face, hiding the wetness of my cheeks. "It's all you."

"No, it's not!" he barked, and I jumped instinctively. "Fuck, Hayne, don't be scared of me. I would never hurt you. You know that. I love you."

"No." My heart thundered from a mix of fear and agony. Mostly pain, although my fight-or-flight reflex had kicked in big-time for a second. Shame there was nowhere to run to. He stood in front of the door, and I couldn't reach the skylights.

"Hayne..."

"I think..." I paused, wet my lips, and swallowed past the choking ball of sorrow in my throat. "I think you should get your stuff and go. I can't get past... you laughing at him whimpering. I just..." I glanced up and was shocked to see tears glistening in his eyes. "I'm reliving every time I've ever been bullied. How can I sleep with someone who can be so cruel? I can't stop the memories, Scott. You have no clue, no idea of what it's like to be... to be me. To be the kid everyone pokes fun at, the kid everyone shoves around. The kid that's held down in the boys' room and has his hair hacked off, or gets whipped with wet towels in the showers after gym, or is ridiculed and slapped and kicked and tripped and... and..." A sob escaped, but I bit back the tsunami of wailing that was coming right behind it.

"Hayne?" he had asked when I had refused to look into those beautiful eyes. "Hayne, please, you have to see that this isn't me."

I lifted my gaze from the hardwood floor. "Are you sure it isn't?"

"Hayne, I love you."

I shook my head, cursed curls falling over my face, tears welling.

"I do, please, just… come on, I need you. I need you to forgive me for this."

"I will just…" I drew in a shaky breath. "I've forgiven lots of people, but I'm not sure I can ever forget the manic glee in your eyes when you… when you…"

"Can you still love me?" he asked, the question a shaky squeak that drove the knife into my heart just a little deeper. Soon it would be protruding from my back.

"I'm not sure."

"Ouch, okay, that's honest. I get it. I love you." He sounded so sincere, so hurt, so desperate for me to forgive him. But I couldn't. Not now. I was too raw, the wound too new. So I shook my head yet again, hugged my middle even tighter, and stood silently sniffling back tears as he gathered some of his belongings and threw them into an OU Eagles duffel bag. "Can you look at me please, just one time before I go?"

My gaze lifted from my toes. Peering into those tortured hazel eyes, I nearly buckled and gave in. I wanted to run to him, kiss him, have him take me to bed, and pretend I'd never seen him being so horrible, but I couldn't. Not yet. Maybe never.

"I'm not taking all my shit, because I'm coming back. When time has passed and the hurt has lessened, we'll talk. Okay? My hockey stuff is going to stay here so that the things that I love the most are in the same place. You good with that?"

"Yes," I squeaked, the flow of tears building.

"I do love you, and I have changed."

I nodded weakly, and he walked out, closing the door behind him. I sank to my knees and let the sobbing commence.

BLUES AND GRAYS. Rain. So much rain. Rain that beat down on the man on the canvas, torrential and unending. It battered his flimsy umbrella, weakening the ribs until the thin spokes bent and the elements doused the man. Me. The man is me.

The man on the canvas is Hayne, and he is drowning in blue and gray…

Lowering my dripping brush, I stared at the painting and sighed. Then I threw it across the studio with a guttural sort of cry that fit the mood that now lay draped over my house like a funeral cloak.

Scott was gone.

My chest tightened.

"No, no more tears," I muttered, spinning to stare at the skylights. Stars at night, millions of them, white pinpricks on an ebony canvas, a clear winter night. No rain fell outside. It was too cold for rain. The deluge was inside, soaking my soul.

The past few weeks had been harrowing. Ever since that video of Scott tormenting Danny had been brought to life, the joy I'd been wallowing in had dried up. Like a spring pond that now sat baking under a brutal summer sun.

I crawled into the bed that Scott and I had shared and looked up at the stars Scott and I used to look at. My stomach snarled in protest, but I ignored the sounds of hunger. How was I supposed to face tomorrow, and my mother and Mimi? How on earth was I going to be able to go to the museum, smile and shake hands and socialize, while *Winter Knight* hung behind me, reminding me of the love that I still harbored for a man who was no longer a part of me? A man who could be so cruel to men like me?

"How?" I gasped, rolled to my stomach, and wept and wailed into the bedding. Sleep was an atrocious beast, clawing at me like a hell hound, ripping and tearing, until I woke up with a snotty nose and red, swollen eyes, the morning still hours away. I rolled to my side, seeking the big, hard body that used to rest there, and finding just a cold blanket. Burying my face into the pillow his head had rested on, I drew the subtle scent of him into my lungs. Then I hugged the pillow hard, crushing it to me, as the replay of our last encounter weeks ago replayed in my mind for the ten-thousandth time.

How he'd come to me that night... the night it had all broken, and had shown me the video that exonerated him, or he claimed it did, and I stood there, listening. Even though agony and drama had dulled me, I still could see how all of this was Craig's fault. Or was it? And that creeping doubt had begun to take root. Like a tenacious weed, it wrapped its tendrils tightly around me, the fears that lived with me, the pain of being bullied for ages because I was small and skinny and had curls and liked boys...

Hunger finally spurred me to rise. I hadn't eaten in... who knew how long. My tiny fridge was empty, and so I had to brave going down to the kitchen. Lank curls dangling in my face, worn jeans, and a T-shirt that needed to be washed as badly as I did, I snuck down the stairs as my stomach roared. Maybe just a PB& J to tide me over or a handful of pretzels.

Stepping into the kitchen, I spied a loaf of bread on the counter and dove on it, taking out two slices and carrying them to the fridge. The inside of the fridge was gross, but there was food. Milk, bologna, cheese, salad, and a bucket of fried chicken. I slapped some bologna on my bread, took a huge bite, and sighed in pleasure. Then I took out the milk and a chicken leg and turned to find a plate.

Craig and Dexter stood in the doorway, neither seemingly happy to see me.

"Dude, we pay for that food. Yours is upstairs," Dexter reminded me. Craig, being the insecure ass maggot that he is, took several steps in my direction. I held up a chicken leg to ward him off.

"Put it back. All of it. And then pay me for the sandwich." He folded his arms over his chest. Dexter did the same. "Well, what are you waiting for, fag? Your fellow fag hockey-playing boyfriend isn't here anymore, is he? What happened? Did you two have a fight over which one was the girl and which was the boy? Did he move out and take all your sissy cakes with him?" He snickered.

I'm not sure what it was about the sound of that derisive little snort, but something inside me snapped. I whipped the chicken leg at Craig, then threw the jug of milk at his big head. Both impacted his forehead within seconds of each other, the jug hurting way more than the chicken leg judging by the grunt of pain.

"Get out. Both of you. Get out now!" I shouted, throwing my sandwich at Craig, as well as a spoon from the sink and a dish sitting on the counter that held a dried-out pickle and four crusts of bread. Dexter jumped back, his eyes as round as the plate that sailed over Craig's fat head. "Get out. Both of you."

"Fuck you, fag." Craig lunged at me, his fingers latching onto my biceps. I wished I still had my chicken leg. Dexter grew a spine then and jerked Craig away from me, his grip on my arm leaving bright red welts. I skittered out of reach, pulled out my phone, and held it in the air. "You better call for help, you faggot."

"If you're not out in ten minutes, I'm calling the police and reporting this incident as a hate crime." That stalled Craig in his tracks. "I'll show them the bruises, and you'll be off this campus before you can spike another person's drink. Now get out. Get out. Get out!"

"Fine, I was tired of living with a cock-sucking little fairy like you, anyway," Craig snapped, jerking free of Dexter and storming up to the second floor.

"Sorry it came to this. Finding a place to crash is going to suck," Dexter muttered before he too climbed the stairs. He never said he was sorry about the abuse that I'd taken from his buddy all year, just that he was put out that he had to find a new place to live. They left after fifteen minutes. I shook for several hours after the front door clicked shut, but my house was mine.

LIFE WAS a miserable kind of void after that one moment of bravery—or madness. Now that the adrenalin rush was over, I couldn't decide which description fit that moment best. It was empty of all life and love and laughter. I left the attic only to go to class and work. I couldn't skip classes, and I could *not* skip work. I needed every penny. I had no roommates now to help cover food and utilities. I begged my manager for more hours. She gave me weekends in the dish room at the campus cafeteria. Fun. Not. But it was money. My gas would stay on for another month, and the lights would still shine in my studio. I'd just not eat outside of work. I got a four-dollar allotment for food a shift. I could live on a sandwich and a pint jug of milk per day.

Now I lay there waiting for the day to dawn, a day that should've been fabulous but was now dismal and dark. Scott's pillow was soft on my cheek, and I drifted off, sleep overpowering me as it did when body and soul were drained.

I woke to someone yelling my name. Torpid and caught in a dream where Scott was dangling me by my heels over a pit of hungry lions—it was far too Roman gladiator—I begged my mother for five more minutes, then fell back to sleep. The next awakening was gentler, the brush of fingers over my brow, the push of springy hair from my cheek, and the soft strains of Saint-Saëns *The Swan* from the *Carnival of Animals* began to play, and I cried softly because only my Mimi played that. She had a key to this place, and evidently she'd let herself in.

"Oh baby boy," she cooed, gathering me into her arms as she had when I was little. Thick arms cinched me to an ample bosom, and I let my cheek rest on her breast, silent tears running down my face. "You let it all out now."

She patted my hair, knowing better than to dig her fingers into the thick curls, as she had hair just like mine. Mimi had tons of them. My father had too; I'd seen his pictures. A tall black man in a crisp police uniform. He'd died when I was four months old in a simple roadside stop that had gone horribly wrong.

"Tell me to toughen up," I begged. Someone had to.

"You'll hear no such shit from me." She patted my head softly, then sat me up, using the sleeves of her brilliant green crocheted sweater to dry my face. "Emotions, like art, must run free."

"I love you." She smiled at me, and the blues and grays seemed to lift just a bit. "I'm taking my pills. I am. It's just too... I still love him."

"Of course you do." She cupped my face between her hands, her fingertips calloused from so many years of playing the violin. The music was working its magic, easing the darkness inside me. I should have turned it on as soon as Scott left, but it reminded me of him, of the paint and silliness and the kisses and caresses...

"Is Mom here?"

"She's unpacking the food we brought for you. I've been instructed to bring you down to eat."

"Blueberry pancakes?"

"Fresh from the griddle." Mimi plastered a kiss on my forehead, then wiped at my brow with her thumb. My stomach roared at the mere thought of Mom's pancakes. "You go shower. Make sure you condition," she said with a patient smile. I nodded. "Then come down. We want to talk to you about... well, things." Her brown eyes darted to the canvasses lying all over, the dour tones of black and blue and gray speaking rather loudly to an ear as well trained as hers.

Thirty minutes later, I was sneaking into the kitchen. My mother smiled at me, placed the platter of enormous pancakes on the recently washed table, and opened her arms. I flew into them, hugging her to me, my breathing growing rushed and thick as she held me tight, the warm scent of soft rose engulfing me.

"Look up here at me," she finally said, holding my face between her hands much as Mimi had. "You are such a beautiful man. So delicate and emotive. Your father would be so proud."

I placed a kiss to her soft, white cheek. "I'm not sure, Mom. I've been hiding from life, from him, from everything…"

"Are you taking your meds?"

"Yes, yes, I am, every day. I just…" My sigh was enormous.

Mom patted my shoulder, then pushed me gently to a chair. "Sit and eat. You've lost weight, and you didn't have any to spare."

She forked five pancakes onto my plate. My eyes widened. Mimi chuckled as Mom then doused the pancakes with syrup. The rich smell of sweet butter and maple danced inside my nose, making my mouth water. They nibbled as I ate. When I was done, the plate was empty and my stomach was huge. Mimi's head bobbed along to Mozart playing from her phone. There was always music where Mimi was. It was one of a billion things I loved about her.

"Now, tell us how you plan to fix your life." Mom took a sip of black coffee, her keen blue eyes locked on me— my face—reading me as easily as one did her lyrical poems.

"I uhm…" I glanced at Mimi. She'd pulled out her crocheting, which meant she was in pure listening mode. Maybe she'd toss in a few "Mm-hmms" here and there.

Mimi jerked her chin at me to goad me on. "I uhm… well, I'm going to go to the museum today with you and Mimi and talk to bloggers and news people. And I promise I'll eat more."

"I know you will. We'll be here for a week to make sure that you're back on track."

I smiled because having them there made me happy. I hated this empty house so much. I missed Scott desperately.

"Mm-hmm," Mimi said as she hooked and pulled yarn with incredible speed. I didn't have time to ask what that sound was for.

"What about this man of yours?" Mom asked, her coffee steaming in front of her little nose. I'd gotten that from her, that tiny nose, and the set of my eyes, the rest of me was pure Gerome Ritter from my curly hair to my tiny toes. Mom had made sure I knew where I came from and where I was going. She guided me with words that I sometimes had to spend hours deciphering. "Have you decided how to take him back into your loving heart?"

"I uhm…" I nibbled on my lower lip. It was sticky and sweet with syrup. "He's… I just, he's capable of being mean to people."

"We're all capable of being cruel, Hayne. The human heart runs to dark, horrid places," Mom replied, lowering her mug to the table. "From what you've told us, this young man needs you now more than ever." I nodded. Curls tumbled over my face to tickle my nose. I left them there, better to hide behind. "People can change, Hayne. See if you can find it in that big heart of yours to offer Scott an olive branch. I sense a love that most would envy in you for this man. And knowing you as I do, I'm certain he loves you with as much passion as you feel for him. How could he not?"

"Mm-hmm," Mimi chimed in as Mozart gave way to Faulkner's *New Beginning,* and I had to wonder if she'd picked this soundtrack beforehand. Knowing her, she had.

―――――

MY SUIT FELT ITCHY, the tie too tight, my slicked-back curls too firmly pasted to my head. Mom and Mimi stood flanking me, smiling and talking to the hundreds of people who had filed into the exhibition to see my painting. My cheeks hurt from grinning, the pancakes from breakfast sat in my belly like a rock, and my head was swimming. The many names, phone numbers, business cards, congratulations, and heaping praises for *Winter Knight* swirled around inside my head. The museum was packed, the air thick with chitchat, perfume, and piano music provided by one of my fellow OU college students.

"… your thesis on?"

I blinked up at the tall man with the long nose. "Oh, uhm, I'm thinking of something that might reflect figure/ground relationships within the parameters of Jung's *Red Book* and symbolic artwork."

"Jung, as in Carl Jung the psychologist?"

I opened my mouth to reply to Mr. Tall Man when Scott appeared to my right, dressed in a finely cut dark gray suit, his hair combed, his cheeks still pink from the razor.

"Ahem? Jung like the—?"

"Excuse me." I gently pushed around Mr. Tall Man, shoving my glass of sparkling pink ginger ale at my mother, and took the fourteen steps to Scott. His gaze traveled over me. I grew hot and hard and giddy all at once. "My knight has arrived."

He blushed at that, his hazel eyes clouding with some deep emotion that made my pancakes feel light as butterflies.

"I thought you might have security throw me out."

"Never. Not ever."

He gave me a crooked smile. The blueberry butterflies took wing. "That's nice to hear. I wanted to come support you, and him." He waved a big hand at the painting. "I miss you," he tacked on quickly, as if hoping to sneak it in.

"I've missed you too."

And then we stood there like two idiots, soaking up the sight of each other. Someone walked by, nudging me into Scott. I threw the clumsy art patron a dark look, then realized it was Mimi, sashaying past in her flowery yellow dress and thick woolen shawl combo, her curls drawn to the top of her head where they flowed downward like a waterfall.

"Would you like to find a bench and talk? Maybe have a drink?" I sputtered, oddly aware of everything all at once.

"No champagne, thanks."

"Oh, there's pink ginger ale. It's sweet as a cherry pop and makes your nose bristle and twitch. What?"

"You're the most incredibly adorable thing ever. I'd really like to find a bench and have some ginger ale with you."

I nearly swooned into his strong arms, but instead I offered him a hand. He slid his palm over mine, causing a massive surge of blueberry butterflies to beat against my breastbone. We went to the bar, spoke to Diana and Professor Poole, and then I led my knight to a rounded cement bench placed under a modern painting of a snowstorm blowing over a lake.

I sipped my bubbly drink, eying him over the rim of the flute. He rolled the stem of his glass between his fingers, his sight darting to me time and again. The piano picked up a lively little waltz tune, something from Strauss that made me long to dance with him once more.

"I wish I hadn't asked you to go," I blurted out and took a tiny taste of my drink.

"Yeah?"

"Oh yeah, I think… I was scared. I still am."

He nodded, his overly long hair brushing the top of his ears. "I get that. I scare myself. I've been doubling up on counseling, missing seeing you at the grief meetings…"

"I couldn't go. I knew you'd be there. And if I saw you, I wouldn't be able to process properly. You make me giddy and airy, stupidly flouncy, and unable to think in tones other than pinks and yellows."

"Those sound like really happy colors." I nodded, and my curls stayed in place. Mimi's hair gel was incredible. He shifted on the bench to face me. "I want to make you happy, I always have, but I'm still working on me. I think I need a lot of work."

"I think you're a canvas with just a blue dot on it." He raised a brow. "Every work begins with a small application of color. With a skilled hand and a gentle brush that droplet of indigo can become a masterpiece."

"I can listen to you talk for hours." He lifted his hand, reaching for a curl, then hesitated. My gaze moved over his face, searching for the truth of Scott as it rested in his eyes and the curve of his lips and the strong line of his jaw.

"Go ahead and pull it free." He smiled and tugged a stiff curl from my skull. It fell down over my eye, lying there like a stick. That made us both chuckle. "If I asked you to come to dinner tomorrow night to meet my mother and Mimi, would you come? Or have I pushed you away for good?"

He toyed with the curl, rubbing it, but the gel was just too powerful. The back of his fingers brushed my cheek. I drew in a breath and waited, on tenterhooks, for him to accept or decline my offer of a fattening olive branch.

"What time?"

The butterflies broke free.

THIRTEEN

Scott

I DECIDED IN THE SPACE OF A FEW SECONDS THAT I WAS going to love Hayne's family. It wasn't any one particular thing, but the way they hugged Hayne, and then me, as if I was worthy of being hugged, left me with the warm and fuzzies. They smiled at me, pulled me into a four-way hug, but it was the way Hayne's mom hugged me again, soft against me, murmuring that everything was okay into my ear.

I was seriously going to lose my shit, break down in front of them, but at least it was just the four of us sitting in Hayne's kitchen and not a crowd of people in a restaurant.

His grandma, Mimi he introduced her as, was wearing the same flowery yellow dress as she had worn last night, silver clips in her corkscrew hair, her lips in a permanent smile. There was humor in her eyes, and she was the one who kicked off the questions.

"So tell us about yourself, Scott," she said, and I

groaned inwardly. That was a pretty wide question, and I wasn't sure where to start.

"Mimi, don't start with the interrogation," Hayne's mom said with a laugh. Her name was Mona, and she said I should call her that, but it didn't feel right on my tongue. I didn't want to disrespect her, so I decided if I needed to call her anything, it would be Mrs. Ritter. She was gorgeous, and I could see her son in her. Her hair was long and blonde, not curly, but I'd seen the wedding photo of Hayne's parents, the small blonde standing next to the tall, striking man in the police uniform. Hayne had come by his soft curls honestly, a mix of his parents, but he'd gotten his dark hair and eyes from his dad.

Mrs. Ritter had cooked tonight, a stew with huge chunks of beef, vegetables and piles of freshly baked rolls, and I was desperate to dive in, but I guess answering Hayne's grandmother's question wouldn't delay eating for very long, because I didn't have a lot to say to Mimi or Mrs. Ritter.

"I'm studying chemistry, in my junior year. I love it."

There, that was enough, and I hoped I would get away with that.

"Eat," Mrs. Ritter demanded, and I rapidly forked up a mouthful of tender steak.

But Mimi wasn't done at all. "So you took drugs to cheat at hockey?"

The steak choked me, and I nearly spat out a mouthful of gravy, coughing and sipping at my water to get ahold of myself. I could argue that wasn't the truth about cheating, but I'd long since come to terms with the fact that actually, yeah, it was cheating to cover up the alcohol abuse and grief with the steroids. I certainly hadn't been honest with my team, my coach, or even myself.

"I was drinking. A lot. I mean, I was drunk most of the time, and I'm not proud of it. Then my hockey suffered, and then I had an easy solution handed to me. The steroids were just another step in addiction."

Own your pain. Monica's soft words were bouncing in my head. I sure was owning my pain right here and now.

"That's just a result," Mimi began, and I heard Mrs. Ritter sigh softly, as if she'd been expecting this. She didn't stop Mimi from talking though, and Hayne smiled at me in sympathy. He surely wouldn't let Mimi go too far and dig too deep, right?

"I'm sorry?" I said when it became obvious she'd paused to wait for me to talk.

"The drinking was to hide something, I guess, and the drugs, well, that was just a way of hiding the drinking. So what was it you were trying to escape?"

I blinked at her. Surely she knew? Hadn't Hayne told her the full story? I had a complicated answer about how I didn't feel right in my own skin, that some days I had felt so black and hopeless that I hadn't wanted to get out of bed, or that I felt as if I was losing my mind.

"My brother died; it was grief." The weight that lifted from me when I finally said the words was immense. I'd never admitted to anyone other than Hayne that I was lost in grief and that I couldn't find a way out.

Mimi considered me for a moment, then patted my hand. "Grief is a terrible thing. When my Gerome died, God rest his soul, it was only because Mona wouldn't let me pull away, made me a strong part of Hayne's life, that I didn't lose my way. When a family breaks apart after a loss, it can leave every person vulnerable, and I'm sorry that happened to you."

So Hayne *had* told her the full story, about Mom and Dad, and everything. I was grateful and annoyed all at the same time. Not annoyed with Hayne, but with Mimi for making me talk about things.

But she got you to admit out loud why you've been so fucked up.

Mrs. Ritter interrupted the quiet face-off between me and Mimi, dropping her cutlery to the table. "I forgot the butter," she announced pointedly, and when she came back to the table, the curious tension was easing. Was it important to Mimi for her to get me to admit my dark parts in front of her daughter-in-law and grandson? Or was she some wise old woman, like the ones in the movies, who knew exactly what to say and when?

We moved on to other subjects then. Hockey, art, school, but the one that got me was when Mrs. Ritter asked me what I wanted to do for a career with a degree in chemistry.

"I have no idea," I blurted. I'd never given any thought to what lay beyond college. I know Dad had wanted me to go the professional hockey route, even if it meant languishing in the lower leagues and never making it to the NHL. Of course, Mom didn't have an opinion either way. "Maybe research or teaching."

Where did those completely viable options come from?

"We always need teachers," Mimi said.

"And people who can find ways to cure diseases," Mrs. Ritter offered.

Yeah, I really liked these two.

They just seemed to care.

THE MELANCHOLY SETTLED in for the long haul after Hayne's family had left. The house was emptier, and the things I'd said with so much confidence to them seemed almost unobtainable in the light of day.

Teacher? Yeah, right. That would mean more education, and I was only funded for the time I had left here at Owatonna. Research chemist? That would take a lot more than what I was capable of achieving right now. I'd fucked up a lot already this year, and unless I pulled myself together, I was done. The thought of that made me low.

Being low made me think my life choices were useless.

Which made the blackness even worse.

Monica called it spiraling, and even though I could see myself doing it, I didn't know how to stop it. I'd even snapped at Hayne for spilling paint on my Eagles jersey. Like I even needed to hurt him right now, for God's sake. And to top it all off, today was my first teaching session at the rink, and I could imagine the hostility from the parents, the screaming kids, Coach staring at me from the sidelines, not to mention that Coach wanted to see me beforehand.

I had to go with paint on my jersey, feeling like a fraud for even wearing the number seventeen on my back when I wasn't part of the damn team. I wish I'd worn my generic Leafs Nation jersey. No one would point at me and shake their heads for that. Unless they weren't a Leafs fan, I guess.

"Shut the door, Scott," Coach said and gestured to the chair in front of his desk. I shut the door, then took the seat, thankful I only had ten minutes or so before I had to be out on the ice. "How are you?"

"I'm good," I lied.

"And the support group?"

"Super helpful."

Coach nodded. "Good, excellent. Okay, now this team of kids..." He immediately bombarded me with stats and reviews and roundups, and I realized he was focusing on the hockey and not on my issues. I tuned back in when he finished what he was saying and turned serious.

"I've talked to the parents, about you making amends and using this experience to connect with the kids, show them that drugs are bad, make them fully aware of their options. You agree with that?"

Of course I had to nod. Not that I wanted to become a walking lesson in what not to do to a bunch of kids.

He rose from his seat, clapped me on the shoulder, half hugged me, and I'm not ashamed to say I accepted the compassion for what it was, and leaned into him.

When I removed my skate guards and took my place on the ice, I collected ten kids, six boys, four girls, and got them all to take a knee. I crouched down with them because hell, they were all really short little people.

Coach had suggested we work on skate skills, so that was where I started. We warmed up with lazy figure eights, from one end of the rink to the other, me in front like a momma with her ducklings, the thought of which made me smile. Every time we passed the top end of the rink, I came face-to-face with a phalanx of hockey moms and dads, and part of me was waiting for them to say something. No one came down and demanded that I stay away from their kid, so I counted that as a win. As we skated, speeding up a little, and then slowing, building up the warmth in our muscles, I turned and began to skate backward, watching the kids skate, seeing in all of them something I'd lost a long time ago: excitement about skating. Warmed up, I set out some small obstacles, including a two-inch jump and a pole to slide under, then added cones to work on corners, and a small container with a flag to indicate change of direction.

They listened to me. Every single one of them looked up at me and listened, and slowly, piece by piece, the blackness slipped away.

One of the boys held back, seeming to be all kinds of uncomfortable, rocking on his skates, and I was careful to keep an eye on him. He was frowning behind his mask, and the way he gripped his stick made me think he was stressing about something. I split them into small groups, rotating one-on-one time and then finally managed to get some time with the kid. Ethan, he said his name was. Ethan, nine, and did I know his big brother Andrew who was six years older than him and was brilliant. His words, not mine.

"Andrew's real good," Ethan said, and I leaned down to listen to him.

"I saw your crossovers. I think you're really good as well."

Ethan looked around as if he was scared someone would hear him. "I can't do the jumps so well."

I crouched in front of him, fussing with the lace of his right skate, so I could whisper my wise words of advice and experience, for what they were worth.

"I couldn't get the hang of the jump for the longest time when I was your age, not until I realized that I was jumping with my feet, and you know what? You need to lift your whole body, feel the jump all the way to your nose."

He blinked at me. "My nose."

I nodded grandly. "Yep, all the way to your nose. You ready to try?"

He glanced from me to the tiny jump and back again. "Sure," he said, sounding anything but. I watched this little kid pull back his shoulders, then wrinkle his nose. He skated for the jump, and I willed him to make it, which he did. Just. His landing was a little wobbly, but the elation I felt that he'd managed to get over that pole was more than I could contain. I high-fived him and touched my gloved fist to my nose.

Right there and then all thoughts of being a teacher or a researcher went out of my head. I could imagine working with kids and their hockey, maybe sleep on Hayne's floor for the rest of my life, living off ramen and canned hotdogs. At least kids and hockey could be fun.

When the kids skated off to get changed, a couple of the dads made their way over to me. Not the moms, they all sat quietly, and I quickly assumed the two men had been delegated to talk to me.

"You got Ethan to jump," one man said and extended his hand. "Nice job. Andrew finds it all so easy, but Ethan has a little fear in him."

Why was he telling me that? Was he likening Ethan to Andrew and labeling him a failure? No fucking way. I bristled.

"Every player has a different journey," I said, and the dad took a step back. I waited for him to argue.

"I know," he said and shook his head ruefully.

"Andrew is so jealous that his little brother is learning it all for new, wishes he could be back here. Between you and me, I think Andrew is finding Juniors overwhelming, and he wants to push harder, but I want my kids to be kids. You know what I mean. But if it means that much to him, then what can I say? So I was going to ask you, do you do private lessons?"

"That was my question as well," the second man said.

I was lost for words. No, I hadn't even thought of something like that.

"We don't have a lot of money to throw around," Ethan's dad said, lowering his voice, "but it means something to my sons. Hockey *means* something."

"I can help them," I said. "No charge, if you can get them to the rink."

Only later, in the shower did I wonder why the hell I said I'd help for no money.

Stupid? Or maybe this was an atonement of sorts.

Whatever it was, I felt positive, and for the first time in the last few days, the blackness was held back enough that I kissed Hayne into the bed and then rolled so he was lying on me.

"Wanna fool around?" I asked and stole a ramen-flavored kiss.

Hayne grinned down at me and kissed me back in answer.

I was lost.

In Hayne.

FOURTEEN

Hayne

_____

SEX WAS NEVER JUST SEX WITH SCOTT. NOT THAT I KNEW what "just sex" was. I'd never had anyone look at me or touch me or taste me as Scott did. He was always gentle and patient, probably sensing my innocent state by the way I trembled at his touch or came far too quickly.

"God, you are beautiful," he whispered as his hands slid up my chest. He plucked at my nipples, the attention turning them from light pink to a dark rose.

I watched my body react to him, the flush of desire making my skin glisten, the flood of blood to my tender nipples and cock. I let him touch and tease, sighing and moaning as he began to play me as a fine musician would a harpsichord. Yes, that was us. Scott the sexual maestro and me, the virginal apprentice.

"Mm, ah… did you know that there's an instrument called a virginal?" I asked because I said stupid things at inappropriate times.

Do we really want to talk about keyboard instruments

from the early baroque period when we have a man's stiff dick resting right between our ass cheeks?

"Uh, nope, did not know that." He grabbed my hips and lifted me, nudging until he could spread his legs. I settled between them, and I could feel the thick shaft nestled between my tightly closed thighs, the velvety head pressing ever so gently on my hole. "Hey, it's okay, relax. Here, come here." He released a hip and pushed his fingers into my hair, easing me forward enough that he could lick into my mouth. I sucked his tongue greedily. He raised his hips just a bit, a mere inch, but oh my God, the sensations that small movement caused. His cockhead rubbed over my asshole, gliding up, then back, the slippery trail of precum that leaked from him easing the friction.

"Oh God, oh God, oh God," I panted, and so he did it again and again, all the while nibbling at my mouth, his tongue sliding over my teeth and lips. "I'm not…" I gasped when his cockhead moved over my hole again. "I'm not sure…" *Words. Make words, Hayne.* "I'm not a well-used harpsichord." That made him chuckle gruffly, then pump a bit faster, which made my words flitter away like sparrows. "No one has ever touched my keys."

"I know," he said, his fingertips roaming over my ribs. "And we're not going there tonight." Disappointment mingled with relief. His dick was impressive, thick as hell, and long. "We are going to play just a bit, though. You okay with that? You want me to play with your ass?"

"Yes, yes, yes, yes, yes."

"Grab the lube." I gave him an uncertain look, my heart thumping madly. "I promise I will not penetrate you with my dick. But we *are* going to need lube. Trust me?"

My mouth dropped to his, the kiss speaking for me. "I do trust you. I love you."

He pushed back the wall of curls curtaining our faces. "I love you too. Reach under the bed, pull out my hockey bag."

Not wanting to know why he carried lube with him, I bent over, his strong grip keeping me in place as I pawed around under my bed. My pinkie snagged the strap, and I pulled the bag out and up onto the bed.

"Get the lube out. There are packets. Side pocket." He never stopped touching me as I searched with shaking fingers until I found strings of condoms and lube. "Good man. Now, get us slicked up. Your dick and mine."

He lay under me, hazel eyes hooded, rough palms now rubbing my ass as I tore open packets and applied clear lube to his cock, then mine.

"Now, we bump and grind." He positioned me as I had been, between his thick legs, his cock locked between my thighs. He thrust up. I bit down on my lower lip and whined in pleasure. "Now you move. Yeah, use your knees. Oh fuck, good, yeah. Nice. Hayne, that's so fucking hot."

I began pumping my hips. He groaned out loud, the sound erotic and beautiful, flowing into the air with the soft strains of *Berceuse in D-Flat Major* as I moved against him. My dick rubbed steadily on his stomach, the friction sending shock waves right to my balls. He spread his legs wider, sliding his hands under his knees. I crossed my ankles and pinched his dick with my thighs.

"Fuck, oh fuck... I'm going to... Fuck." He grabbed my ass cheeks with both hands, his legs falling back to the bed. "Faster. Fuck, Hayne, that's perfect. Faster." He bit down on my shoulder, his steamy breath blowing past my right ear. My balls drew up tight when he closed his legs and thrust up like a man possessed, his fingers holding my ass. The hot wash of cum on my hole sent me over as well. My cock kicked and spewed, coating our bellies with spunk. I whimpered as my release rocked me to the core. Then he touched my ass with a slick finger. I shouted and pumped my hips, using my thighs to milk more out of him. He rubbed at my hole as I shot another thick wad.

"Oh God." It was all I could think of to say. I lifted my ass just a bit, to get more of his finger into me, but he pulled it away. "I want more…"

"Next time," he whispered, his lips skimming over my damp cheek to my mouth.

The kisses were soft now, like the dulcet notes bouncing around the attic. I never wanted to leave this bed or his arms. My head fit perfectly under his chin. I was a mess. Cum coated my ass, balls, thighs, cock, and chest. Scott wasn't much tidier. Yet we lay there with the stars twinkling above us and Chopin on the stereo, kissing and telling each other the things that lovers say in the dead of night after the lust has been spent. Eventually, we'd have to get up, wash up, and change the bedding, but right now, we were still in that place where two are one, hearts entwined. It was where I wanted to live the rest of my life.

A FEW WEEKS LATER, I glanced up from my thesis paper to see Ryker Madsen dragging his backside into Cream the Beano.

"Coffee, stat," he groaned.

I motioned in the general direction of the coffee pots,

then remembered that I was at work. My customer service skills had taken a massive hit the past few weeks.

"I'll get that for you," I offered, but he waved me off, leaving me to stare at my paper, which was due in exactly two weeks. As was my senior project painting and the paper that I had to turn in for my senior seminar class, and finals needed to be studied for, amid working and trying to spend time with Scott, and house-hunting, and filling out applications for full-time jobs nearby. Not to mention getting ready for commencement which was May 10th.

I must have made a sick little sound because Ryker turned from the pot that held the regular coffee to give me a sympathetic look.

"I heard that exact same sound from Jacob last night." He poured himself a tall cup, then fixed it to taste as I sighed, sighed, and sighed again. "Let me guess. Senior thesis?" I nodded at him as he sat down across from me, blowing into his coffee, his pretty eyes puffy and rimmed with red. "I figured. Jacob's is something about a base model in evaluating the amino acid profiles when feeding soybeans or something like that."

"That's horrifying," I replied.

Ryker nodded and took another sip. "What's yours?"

"Oh, it's a paper on the reflect figure/ground relationships within the parameters of Jung's *Red Book* and symbolic artwork."

His face went blank. "Okay, now *that* is horrifying."

I giggled a bit, the first time I'd done that in the past two hours. "You want to talk about scary, listen to the requirements." I cleared my throat and did my best Professor Tritchie impersonation. "Your paper must be word-processed, double-spaced, one-inch margins, twelve-point font Times New Roman only. No silly fonts will be accepted. It must be spelling and grammar checked," I said, in a deep, nasally way that made Ryker snort. "Name and page number on each page, each paragraph numbered, and you *must* write your thesis statement in bold. Cite all your sources, make sure to include a bibliography/works consulted page. Careful and considerate citation is critical!" I shouted, and Ryker laughed out loud. "Your paper must be at least twelve pages long; fifteen to twenty pages would be preferable, but twelve will get you a passing grade if all other points are met."

"C's get degrees," Ryker tossed out. "You got to APA format all that?"

"My God, I don't know. Maybe?" I began to scour the paper requirements for the formatting. Ryker slid it away from me, putting an arm on it, then dazzling me with a killer smile.

"Had to do the same thing for Jacob last night at three in the morning." I blinked at him, then what he was doing settled in, and I gave him a weak smile.

"Thanks. I'm feeling majorly overwhelmed," I confessed, pulling my wild hair back into a thick ponytail.

"Yep, I feel you. Jacob is freaking out. He's got slight control issues anyway, but this final push to graduation is making him two shades shy of a lunatic. Honestly, I'm kind of worried he's going to burn out."

"What's your paper on?" I inquired as two girls came in to grab some candy and milk before classes. I rang them up helped myself to a cup of coffee, and sat back down with Ryker.

"I'm a junior, so I'm skipping it all until next year." He peeled off his Eagles jacket, exactly the same kind that

Scott wore, and tossed it onto the bench next to him. "My only concern this year is what I'm going to do next year without Jacob here."

I could see the sadness in his expression. "Yeah, I kind of get that. I'm looking at six weeks at my current house, and then I have to move out. Grampa's money is about gone. I also need a job, like a full-time one with benefits because making a living as an artist is a pipe dream."

"Dude, no, it's not. Your stuff is good. We all saw that winter painting when it was in the museum. You could totally make a go at painting."

"Yeah, no. And I'm not willing to cut off and sell my ear, not yet anyway."

"Hey, listen, I'm serious. All you'd need is a website and an online store. Easy-peasy setup. Then you sell your paintings online, skip the museum shit, and roll around in cash."

I stared at him. Hard. "What happens when I don't sell any?"

Ryker sighed dramatically. "You *will* sell them because they're good."

"But I won't have a studio because I have to move. And where will Scott go to live? How can I paint when I'm working sixty hours a week to survive? Why did I pick such a prick of a subject for my thesis?! Ack, why is my life like this!?"

"Dude, breathe before you pass out."

My head hit the table and stayed there, forehead thumping from the impact. "Did I mention we have to move?"

He patted my head. "Yeah, do did, twice. Life is a big boner at times."

I sat up. "Yeah, it is. So, what's going to happen with you and Jacob during the summer? Do you live near him?"

I poked at my coffee with a red plastic stirrer. I didn't really want it. I'd taken in so much caffeine in the past two days I was getting queasy, but there was so much to do...

"No, he's here in Minnesota, and I'm going to be with my dad in Harrisburg this summer. He's getting married, and then I'm on house watch while Ten and him are honeymooning. Then there's summer hockey camp, and BLAM! I'm back here on campus alone."

"Maybe Jacob can come stay with you at your dad's." I pushed the coffee away after taking a tentative sip.

"Not likely. Farm work doesn't include vacations. Cows have to be milked and fed every day, crops need to be harvested. I'm hoping to go to him as often as I can, but... I don't know. It's going to suck."

My head bobbed. Yes, it did. "What are we going to do about Scott?" I ran the tip of my index finger over the edge of my laptop, which had gone dark from nonuse. Ryker lifted an eyebrow. A rush of people filed into the coffee shop, the between-classes surge. Ten minutes later, after I'd made more coffee, I was back at the employee table under the TV that was bolted to the wall. It was muted and locked on CNN, so no one ever glanced at it.

"You asked me about Scott. What do you mean what are we going to do with him? Is he using again?"

"No! Oh, sorry, no, he's clean. I just... what are we going to do with him? Where will he go for the Summer?"

Ryker shrugged, his face a mask of sorrow. "I wish I knew, Hayne. Maybe I could ask my dad if he could stay with us, but he really should try to make amends with his family, you know?"

My eyes closed on my exhale. When I opened them, Ryker was waiting, his coffee sitting beside mine, both half full.

"I'm not sure he's there yet, emotionally. We don't talk much about his family. Mine is cool and would totally take us in, but I'm not willing to burden my mother and grandmother like that. I'll be twenty-three in July. I should be able to live on my own."

"Yeah, well, that was the standard for our grandparents' generation. Most of my friends would be happy to have an apartment and some cash left over for food. Life is hard for our generation."

I knew that Ryker came from money. His father had played professional hockey, and his dad's fiancé did as well. Even people like me who knew nothing about sports knew Tennant Rowe's name. To hear him speaking with such feeling about those who didn't have it as well as he did said a lot about him as a man. I had nothing to say and no solutions for any of our problems.

"Well, I better haul it over to the rink. We have a scrimmage today, then a game on the weekend," he said, pushing to his feet and sliding his arm into a coat sleeve. "We're going to do Chinese tomorrow night, just to get Jacob outside for an hour before his brain leaks out of his ears. Want to join us?" I began to beg off, but he wasn't allowing that to happen. "It's OU students eat for half price at the buffet place down on Spangler and March in town. I'll swing by around seven."

"Okay, sure that'll be nice." I smiled warmly up at Ryker.

He swatted my shoulder playfully. "Cool. And listen,

about life and all that? Things have a way of working out. Ten tells me that all the time."

Off he went in a hurry, jogging out of the coffee shop, shouting a greeting to someone he knew. My phone buzzed, and I smiled to see a quick text from Scott. He was working with the kids and sounded upbeat and full of energy. His next text was temptation personified.

Come to the rink.

Why?

I miss you.

I miss you too. My paper is sickly and needs help.

I'll help you at home. Come on, you know you want to…

Ugh, I did. I so wanted to. I loved sitting in the seats and watching Scott on the ice. He was so strong and graceful, a masculine mix that made me tingle from head to toe. I glanced at the clock over the door. Twenty minutes until I could close up. If I hurried to the rink, I could spent an hour there, and then went right home and got to work. I hit him back.

See you in 30.

YASSSSSSSSSSSSSSSSSSSSSSSSSS!!

Scott's reply made me laugh. Filled with an energy I hadn't felt before, I hustled around, washing pots and scouring counters. As soon as the hour hand clicked onto the five, I was tallying up my register, and I was out the door, paper still unwritten. I bounded out into an April afternoon, the air cool but with that gentle caress of spring riding the chill.

Bag bouncing off my back, I ran to the ice rink, waving at several Eagles players who were filing in for the scrimmage game. Scott met me at the door, sweeping me up and twirling me around until I screamed and pretended to gag.

"God, you're pretty, even when you're turning green," he teased, pecking me on the lips, then leading me to my usual seat behind the Eagles bench. "We're going to be out there for another half hour. Then the team comes on. You okay with that?"

"Yep." I patted my backpack resting on my thighs. "I might work on my thesis a bit if that's okay?"

He dropped into a crouch, his fingers taking and tugging a stray curl. "As long as you're nearby. That's really all that matters." He released the strand, and it bounced back into a corkscrew. The kids on the ice shouted his name, and his eyes lit up. "Work. We'll walk home, and I'll make us dinner."

"Ramen or tater tots with cheese?"

"It's a surprise." Off he went, moving far more gracefully than a man should in ice skates with clunky plastic green covers on the blades. Funny, but when I opened my laptop and inhaled that brisk icy air, my fingers began to fly over the keys. Glancing up from time to time, I spied Scott with his young skaters and felt a kind of serenity settle in my breast. The man really *was* my inspiration.

FIFTEEN

Scott

I WATCHED HAYNE AS HE CHECKED HIS WORK ONE LAST time. Looking at him was relaxing and gave me time to think. I'd woken in the middle of the night, a nightmare chasing me from sleep, and Hayne had been hunched over his laptop, muttering. Something about symbolic artwork, or who knows what, I couldn't make sense of it. So I lay there and watched him and thought a whole lot about nothing until I settled on my last counseling session. Monica was an angel, giving me private time, even though I couldn't pay her or anything. She'd made me see so much, talked about something she referred to as my story, and how I just needed to get the narrative fixed and everything could begin to make sense. She never once promised me everything was going to be okay, and that was the right thing, I think.

She'd talked me through all my options, and lying there, I realized I wanted to talk to Hayne about the decisions I was ready to make. He was part of my story, and I owed him an explanation.

"It's done," Hayne said, shutting his laptop, then triumphantly punching the air.

"All of it?" I kissed the top of his head, and he butted up against me like a cat.

"In the cloud. Backed up three times. Every. Single. Word. Fourteen beautiful, sexy, double-spaced pages of cleverness."

"Do you want to go to the library and get it printed right away?" I yawned widely, glancing at the clock. I'd been awake for a couple of hours now, but it was still only six a.m., and the library wouldn't be manned for another hour. Although privately I imagined there were a whole bunch of seniors still there working overnight on last-minute panic-driven submissions. I resolved that I wouldn't be one of those, and that I would have my thesis finished well in advance.

Just like I'd promised myself when I was younger that I would always do my school homework the night it was set. Yeah, that didn't happen when I wanted to play hockey instead. Although at least now I was focused on a subject I loved rather than things that didn't interest me. Maybe that would motivate me to get things done ahead of time.

"It's not open yet," he said and flopped down on the bed, lying spread-eagled and staring up at the window. "I feel…"

He evidently didn't have the words to explain how he felt, so I immediately straddled him and began to help.

"Happy?"

"No. Well, yes, of course I'm happy about finishing and happy in general," he qualified and frowned as he said it. This wasn't the first time I'd seen him worrying, but up to now, I'd laid the blame for it on end-of-year stress.

"Worried?" I gave him another option, and this time he closed his eyes and frowned so hard. "Hayne, what's wrong? Talk to me."

He shook his head, and I kissed him gently, which ordinarily made him smile. Fear gripped me. Was he worried about his work, or was this something to do with me? Was he breaking this off? Was he done? Why was my traitorous brain immediately imagining the end of us? Suddenly straddling him seemed an embarrassing position, and I moved a little to leave him alone, and he sat bolt upright and clung to me. So tight I'm sure I'd have nail marks in my back.

Something was wrong with Hayne, and I wondered if it was just post-thesis letdown. I eased him away, but he wasn't crying. If anything, he looked angry, and he was still holding tight, so he clearly wanted us close, so this wasn't about us or me specifically.

"It's you," he forced out.

Well, shit, it *was* about me.

"What? Did I do something wrong?"

"No, but what will *you* do now? I'm finished, it's all done, and we won't have a home, and even ramen will be too expensive, and then it won't be fun anymore, and you'll meet someone else and—"

I pressed a finger to his mouth and eased away, sitting cross-legged facing him. This wasn't a new worry of his. The thought of what happened next for us was constantly on his mind, and he spoke of it often. I wanted *us* to be a forever thing. At least that is what I wanted to work toward. I loved Hayne, and I knew he loved me, but what about the other stuff, the steroids, the counseling, the hockey kids, me going back to the team if I could, and his painting? How were all these tiny jagged parts of our two different puzzles ever going to fit together? He was waiting for me to say something, and I could just tell him everything was going to be okay, but I didn't know that for sure, and I'd come to certain decisions in the last few hours that I needed to talk over with someone.

Why not Hayne? He's the best listener I know and part of it all.

"The way I see it is this. We're two separate stories…" He let out a small sound of distress, and I realized immediately that was *not* the way to begin this discussion. "No, what I mean is, you have your future, and I have mine, and somewhere in there, our futures are tangled together, in a good way." I added the last part because he clearly thought I was working up to something terrible. "Your art is you."

He blinked at me. "Okaaay."

"God, that makes no sense. Hang on…" I closed my eyes and held out my hands, and he took them and held tight as I desperately tried to recall the things I'd said in my last session. Back at that moment when everything had clicked into place for me to decide, the words had come easy. They weren't now.

"Okay, it's like this." I opened my eyes and met his wary gaze. "You've only known troubled Scott, right? The jock who still can't come to terms with everything, who messed up badly so that he'd be noticed by a dad who wanted him to succeed in the very thing he was fucking up. I want to play hockey again, if I can, and I want to be the best chemistry graduate Owatonna has ever had, and I want to have a career that matters, and one day, I want my story to be all up and entwined with yours for the longest time possible. But my story isn't at the same place as yours. Do you understand? Am I making any sense?"

Hayne shook his head. "Is this you breaking up with me?"

Shit.

"God, no, I just have to do one of two things, and it's all simple if you think about it. Next year, I have nowhere to live, and maybe you won't either, but if I spoke to my dad, talked to him man-to-man, made him see he does still love me, then maybe I could move home, and you could come with me."

His mouth fell open, and I read the horror in his expression. Hayne Ritter in the weirdly toxic environment of my parents' house wasn't something I ever wanted to see either.

I pressed ahead before he could say anything. "I don't want to write my parents off, because they lost a son, the same way I lost a brother. In Luke, they had perfection. Dad could push him hard, Mom would hug him and spoil him, and then he was gone."

"They had another son," Hayne defended.

"Yeah, well, if they really want to cut me out, then the other way is to be entirely clinical, talk to my dad, man-to-man, ask him to help me pay for housing, make it a loan I pay back, get him to see the kind of money I could make using my chemistry degree, come up with a payment schedule for the whole thing, even sign legal documents on repayment. If I had enough for a room in a house, you could share with me, and who knows, maybe we can get an attic with a window to the sky."

"Scott—"

"Either way, you see what I have to do. I need to get

my story back on track by seeing my parents, or the only other choice I have is to leave Owatonna with nothing resolved, and then our stories might never cross the right way, and you might hate me."

"Never!"

I kissed him quickly. "Also, I've been talking to Monica, and she's all about *manifestations of grief*, parents pushing away remaining children after a bereavement. She puts it in all this pretty language, but she said something yesterday that won't leave me alone. She said that my parents must have love in there for me, but I need to make them show it, and if they can't, then I need to start again and find a family that will love me for who I am and what I did. Dad threw me out, but he said he couldn't watch another son die. So if I show him…"

Hayne nodded then. "Scott, you didn't do anything. Luke wasn't your fault."

"Rationally, I know that, but it's a lot to come to terms with, okay?"

"So our schedules today then? I'm going to print out my work in the library," Hayne began. "And you?"

I entwined our fingers. "I need to talk to Mom and Dad."

"Today?"

"Right now."

He smiled at me, kissed me, and then huffed. "We should shower first. Together."

I EXPECTED everything to have changed at my parents' house, given I'd been away for months. But the fountain in the circular driveway still splashed water at me as I passed, windows sparkled as they always used to, and really, the only thing I noticed that was different was the realty sign at the start of the drive. Chloe Baker of Baker & Hull was the person to contact for viewing.

My parents are moving away from Owatonna? Are they leaving me?

This didn't look good for a touching family reunion, and for the longest time I hesitated to knock. I still had a key, but the thought of using it, of walking into a place that didn't feel like mine was awful. What if I walked in, and Mom was there, and she ignored me, or Dad was sitting at his desk, and he ordered me to leave? At least this way, they invited me in or not, and I waited with my shoulders back, my chin tilted, and all the words in the world waiting to spill out.

Dad opened the door, and his eyes widened. "Scott." He peered behind me as if he expected someone to be with me. "Is Hayne with you?"

"Hayne?" What? How did he know about Hayne?

"Your boyfriend, that's Hayne, right? Did I get it wrong?"

"No, that's who he... how did you know about Hayne?"

He pressed his lips together, then huffed out a breath. "I heard some of the boys talking on the bus to the last game. They like him, say he's an artist."

"Yeah."

"Your mom and I looked into him and went to visit the exhibition where his painting was. He's very talented."

"You did?"

He nodded, and we were still in the doorway staring at each other, awkward silence between us.

"Come in," he said like it had just occurred to him I was outside. "Did you lose your key?"

I bristled. "No, Dad, you said I wasn't welcome here, so forgive me if I don't feel like using my damn key."

Shit, I'd never planned to start this with negativity or an argument. That wasn't how this was supposed to go. I'd resolved to talk calmly, rationally, lay out my case, agree to reparations, make things halfway right. Not argue.

But he crumpled. Right in front of me, he backed away until he was at the stairs and he sat down heavily. I went inside and shut the door behind me. *What the hell is going on?* In the hall light, I got my first good look of Dad, and he was tired and gray. Was he okay?

"I never meant to say any of that to you," he began, and my simmering temper flared.

"Leaving me with my bags in the middle of a parking lot was deliberate, Dad. Don't tell me you didn't mean what you did and said."

He closed his eyes, and abruptly I didn't want to be there anymore. I wasn't ready to listen to him talk shit. I wanted more than that from him. I backed away, shaking my head. What was I thinking, coming here with a well thought plan, when my old home contained nothing but chaos and sadness?

"He was scared," my mom said from the doorway, startling the hell out of me. I turned to face her and blinked in astonishment. Her eyes were bright, her shoulders back, her tone certain. This wasn't the mom who'd lost herself to medication and drink after Luke died. This was the mom I remembered from when I was younger. "Your father let me grieve for so long, Scott, that he forgot to mourn for himself, and that day, when he packed your stuff so he didn't have to watch you hurt yourself? That was the lowest day."

"It couldn't have been, Mom. He spent all of Christmas telling my friends I didn't want to see them."

She took a step closer to me and held out a hand. "No, it was the lowest point for me, and when I reached the bottom, it was like a switch in my brain. I stopped drinking, talked to my counselor about the medication, came to terms with things I'd never confronted, and only then did your dad actually have time to grieve."

I took her hand, but it felt odd because displays of affection from her had been few and far between for the longest time. The first thing I noticed was that she wasn't shaky, her grip was steady, and she tugged me close for a hug. Initially, I resisted because none of this felt natural until she had her arms around me, and I bent to hug her back. She was tiny, but she was strong, and she held me so tight.

"Scott, I'm sorry I let you down," she murmured.

"It's okay, Mom," I lied because everything was still too raw.

She stepped back and rubbed my arms. "Come on, you two, I'll make breakfast." Then she walked through to the kitchen.

Dad looked at me; I looked at Dad. What now?

"It was my fault," Dad said and used the banister to stand up. He appeared shaky and older than I'd ever seen him. "If I hadn't been so hard on Luke, if I hadn't pushed him... he wouldn't have left that weekend."

"No, Dad, it was my talking you into it."

He shook his head. "Nothing you said changed my mind. Luke and I, we had a deal." He closed his eyes and rubbed at his chest, his voice hitching with emotion. "I didn't want him to go. There were scouts at the next game, and I wanted him in top form, but he said if he didn't go away, he'd give up hockey. He stood up to me, and I allowed him to go." He collapsed back onto the stairs. "But I told him that if he ever thought he wanted to give up hockey, I never wanted to see him again." Tears slid from his eyes. "I told my son that, and he never came back."

My face was wet. I knew I was crying. I wondered if the ball of grief and pain in my chest would end up killing me. All I could think was that maybe if Dad and I worked through our guilt together, then we could both find some kind of peace.

Maybe we could remake this family.

I took his hand, and we hugged briefly before I pulled away.

"Let's go, Dad. Drink coffee, eat pancakes, and start to make things right."

SIXTEEN

Hayne

I'D NEVER BEEN MORE ON EDGE THAN I WAS THAT NIGHT. I was also proud. Proud of Scott and the progress he'd made in his recovery. But anxiety was overwhelming me. Would his parents slam the door in his face again? Would he stagger off, lost and broken, and get high somewhere? Would he die in some alley? I made another lap around the attic, bare feet slapping the floor in perfect time to Vivaldi's *Summer* pouring out of paint-smeared speakers. Passing my palette table, I paused, my sight touching on tubes of earthy colors as the high tone of a singing violin made my skin break out in goose bumps.

"Yes, I see," I murmured to the colors. I threw a canvas onto the easel and hurried to remove caps from paint tubes. Little white tops rolled to the floor, unseen, unheard, my fingers squeezing dollops of cadmium red, raw sienna, deep forest green, and iridescent bronze to the porcelain tabletop. Medium yellow joined the greens and browns. Ebony and slate for the sky. I lifted a fan brush from one of several cans of well-used brushes. Lashes drifting downward, I breathed in the music and let it coalesce with the tumult inside me. Then, with a stroke of brush through a slick mound of gray, I went to my toes and began working in the sky. Clouds thick and dark, ominous, heavy with rain appeared before me. Grabbing an artist's knife, I then carved jagged arcs into the stormy sky. Then I went for the yellow paint, smearing it into the marks the knife had made. The colors blended. I didn't care. That was fine.

I threw browns on and greens, whipped them into trees, and then ran a fat brush over them, bringing the wind from the music into the painting, spinning and twirling the paint on the canvas as the summer storm assaulted the land. I could smell the scent of rain on the air, feel the charge in the air on my skin, taste the force of a thunderstorm on my tongue. Red then leaped into the clouds, a touch of godhead observing the earth as he pummeled it with rain, wind, and lightning. Paint dribbled off my brushes to my bare toes, but there was no time to stop and wipe it off. Music and color possessed me, and I painted, uncaring of the world that spun around me, the strokes of the brush inching me closer to a completion that was like an orgasm. Was Scott in the middle of a familial storm such as this? Would he be washed away in a deluge of agony?

"You're amazing," Scott said, startling me from the grip of my muse enough to make me spin to look at him. His lips pulled into an adoring smile as he closed the distance. "I love seeing you caught in your art. Look at you." He cradled my face in his hands. I gazed into the most beautiful blue-green coloration only nature could create. No mere man could replicate the glory of Scott's eyes. Oh, I wish we could. "Your pupils are blown out, your skin is flushed, your hair is free and wild, and you're panting. It's like watching you when we make love. Is that how it feels? This artistic rush you get?"

"Yes... in a way." I threw my brush onto my sloppy table and went to my toes to kiss him. "Take me to bed, now, please." I ground my cock into his, thrilled to my marrow to find him as hard as I was. "Love me."

"I do," he whispered before covering my mouth with his. I wrapped myself around him, allowing him to ease me from the floor and carry me to bed, my weight never causing him any strain. He peeled my clothes off and loved me as I had begged him to do. With touch and taste, he got me to the summit, his grip firm on my cock as he stroked me to completion, his own release coming directly after mine, our mouths joined, our bodies straining and damp with exertion.

He lay down beside me, *Summer* feeding naturally into *Autumn* on the stereo, and wiped off his chest and my belly with the shirt he'd taken off my back not all that long ago. I curled tightly against him, like an old cat seeking warmth, and he tugged the sheet over us.

"That was incredible." I sighed, tracing the dark disc of his nipple with my finger, leaving a tacky dot of gray paint on the rigid nub.

"Always. It's always incredible with you." He rolled his head to kiss my curls. "My dad and mom..."

I held my breath.

"They took me in. We talked. It was, uhm, it was nothing as...... I'd thought or was expecting. It was good."

Tears welled, but I willed them away. "I'm so happy. So, so happy!" I kissed his chest, his side, and then I buried my face in his armpit and kissed him there. He snorted at the ticklish brush of lips to pit hair, tugging me away from that tender area with a firm but gentle hand on my arm. I snuggled into his side, inhaling the trace of soap on his skin that mingled with the smell of sex.

"Yeah, it's good. I think it's going to work out. They're moving, though. I didn't know why that kind of shocked me, but I get it. The house is too big and too full of memories."

"Mm, I understand that." I thought of Jay-Jay's mom and dad, alone in that big house with nothing but recollections of their son and a life they no longer had. "I wish people we love didn't have to die. I miss Jay-Jay so much at times. You would have liked him. He was brilliant and funny and chivalrous. Always standing up to bullies for me, helping me through the dank, disgusting pit that's high school. He was a good friend who deserved a much longer life."

"I know I would have liked him because he loved and shielded you." Another kiss to my curls. I sighed dreamily, sinking into his side, the familiar rousing strains of *Winter* fading as sleep crept up on me. "What were you painting?"

"Storm, gods, upheaval, strife. I was worried about you."

"You can stop worrying, babe. It's all going to be okay."

I drifted off in his arms, the storm having passed.

THE NOT WORRYING about things lasted exactly two days. Handing in my thesis and my senior independent work painting—which turned out to be *God's Wrath*, the storm painting that was still damp to the touch in some places—set off anxiety that was compounded as final exams began a mere ten days later. I studied, cried, studied, curled into a ball in Scott's arms, and simpered into his throat for a solid week. The one time we ran into the guys, the hockey guys that is, as I had no guys, Ryker looked exhausted, and Jacob appeared to have been tossed into a hay baler.

"My brain is toast," the big farmer moaned, his forehead dropping to the table at the The Aviary that had become our hangout over the semester. I reached over and patted his head.

"I can sympathize," I said, then lifted a cup of decaf blueberry tea to my lips. Mimi had sent it to us because I was known to get antsy—her words not mine. Ryker and Scott and Ben just stared at us, wide-eyed, knowing that they were all next in line to feel the senior crush.

Just as the insanity of finals ended, my landlord called to tell me that he was selling the house and that he'd be by on Saturday with a couple who wanted to invest. That set off a whole new round of stress that nothing, not Mimi's blueberry tea or Scott's neck rubs, could alleviate. We rushed around cleaning, fretting all the while because we had nowhere to go once classes were done for the summer.

"If we'd known this earlier, I could have asked my folks to let us live in the pool house," Scott said the morning the potential buyers and my landlord were due to arrive. The house smelled good, of lemons, and it was as clean as we could get it. There were things that showed wear and tear. Fresh paint was needed in several rooms, and the carpet on the stairs was worn bare in spots, but that was up to the new owners, not us as renters. "But they're moving into a condo, and there's no extra room."

"No, no, it's it's fine." I dusted off the TV for the tenth time in five minutes. "if push comes to shove, we'll move in with Mimi and Mom. I hate to do that but—"

The front door opened, and I bit down on my lower lip. Scott walked over to me, looped an arm around my neck, and pulled me close.

"Everything will be okay," he whispered as Mr. Binkes, my elderly landlord, stepped into view, his bald head as shiny as ever.

"Oh, here they are," Mr. Binkes said with a toothless smile and tottered into the living room, two big men walking in behind him. Scott made a choking sound. I blinked up at him, worried that he was having some sort of fit, given the clicking sounds he was making. "This is—"

"Scott and Hayne, yes, we've heard a lot about you two," the older man said and offered his hand to Scott. I wrinkled my nose in confusion. Scott gabbled and grinned as he shook the hand of the big blond man, then moved to clasp hands with a dark-haired guy around my age. "Ryker was the one who told us about your housing situation."

"Uhm?" I weakly said, hoping for some clarification of things.

"Oh, these are Jared Madsen and Tennant Rowe," Scott said, then looked at me as if that were all the information I needed. I raised a brow. "Ryker's father and future stepdad. They play hockey for the Railers. Hayne, dude, we talk about Ten all the time."

"No, hey, it's cool. Nice to meet someone who's not looking for an autograph," the young man, Tennant, said, then offered me his hand. It was huge, but then again most of the hockey players I'd gotten to know had massive mitts.

Neither one of them seemed like big-name sports stars. There was no ostentatious jewelry to be seen, just slim bands on their ring fingers. They wore super casual jeans, T-shirts and jackets. Pricey sneakers on Tennant Rowe's feet, though.

"We're looking to diversify some cash before we get married, so a rental property near campus for Ryker sounded like a good investment. Will you two be staying here over the summer? If we buy, we'll need someone to take care of the place until fall when Ryker moves in. He's expressed some concern about living alone without Jacob here and said something about you two probably renting the attic come Fall…"

Ryker's dads were trying to make him less lonely come fall. I'm convinced that was something that my mom or Mimi would've done if they'd had money to diversify.

"We… uhm… sure. Yes. We'd love to stay!" I replied in a voice a pinch too high for human ears. "I mean yes, we'd love to be house sitters over the summer."

Jared nodded, Ten smiled, and Mr. Binkes led them off to explore the rest of the house.

"See," Scott said, pressing a kiss to my lips. "I told you things were going to work out."

"I guess so," I replied, then grimaced when someone turned on the radio in the kitchen and *Waltz of the Flowers* blared to life. Scott laughed into my hair, spun me around, and led me through a horrible waltz where we stumbled and stepped on each other's feet until the volume was lowered and Tennant Rowe was yelling out apologies for cranking up the Mozart jams.

"It's not Mozart," I began to shout back, but Scott cut that off with a brisk kiss.

"He doesn't really care, babe."

I started to say that people should care if a song was written by Mozart or Tchaikovsky, but he just kept kissing snobby classical music me into submission until I stopped talking and hung off him and licked back into his sweet, hot mouth.

That was how the landlord and Misters Madsen and Rowe found us when they returned to check the thermostat in the living room. Me draped over Scott's arm as he sucked on my tongue.

Face feeling as red as an apple, I hid behind Scott for the rest of the tour. As soon as the door shut on the back of my landlord, Scott chased me up to the attic, pinned me to the bed, and kissed me all over several times, making me squeal, groan, and then howl in pleasure.

Maybe things would work out after all…

Epilogue

SCOTT

LUKE'S BIRTHDAY IS ALWAYS A BAD DAY. HE WOULD HAVE turned twenty-six this year, and maybe by now he'd be out there living the dream, playing in the big leagues. He could have been a dad by now, or a bachelor with a string of girls on his arm. He could have been on television, interviewed, a whole mess of fans wanting to know him.

I think that was the hardest part of today, listing all the possibilities and knowing he would never see any of them happen.

Hayne came with me to the cemetery, holding my hand and only dropping it when he saw my parents were already there.

"I'll stay here," he murmured and stopped walking. I only took a single step before I stopped and extended my hand to him.

"I want you to be with me, if that's okay."

"Really?" he peeked past me at where my parents stood, and bit his lip. "Does that seem right?"

I wasn't sure if there was anything in this world that

could be more right than us holding hands and sharing time with Mom, Dad, and Luke. I tugged him to get him to come with me, and finally he acquiesced, staying close to my side and staying super quiet.

Luke was buried in a serene place, a corner of the graveyard under the canopy of a tree that dropped golden leaves every fall to keep him warm and brightened his sky every spring with emerald green. Mom had chosen the spot, told me at the funeral that she wanted to be with him in the same place. I thought she would have left me by now, scared to face the world without him. But she hadn't. She was still here, still my mom, and even through her tears, she smiled at me and pulled me into a hug.

"It's good to see you," Dad said and hugged me after, then held out a hand to Hayne. "Hello. It's Hayne, right?"

Hayne shook his hand, all formal, and stiff-backed. "Yes, sir."

"Call me Gordy, or Gordon," he said without pause. "Gordy is... was my hockey nickname, and this is Melanie, my wife, Scott's mom."

Then it was Mom and Hayne, and tears spilled as she cupped Hayne's face. "Oh my," she breathed. "I'm so pleased to see Scott in love. You are beautiful." She tugged at one of his curls, and he gave her a shy smile. "What I wouldn't give to have your curls."

I took Hayne's hand again. "Come and meet Luke."

Dad stood to one side, and then he and Mom backed away, to give us a private moment.

"Hey, Luke," I laid my hand on the smooth marble, then crouched down in front of the simple words. "Luke Caldwell, aged twenty-one. Beloved son and brother. Taken by the ocean. Forever in our hearts." I read them quietly, and Hayne went to his knees on the grass next to me, tracing the letters. He looked at me uncertainly, then cleared his throat.

"Hello, Luke. I'm… I don't know what to say…"

"Tell him who you are," I encouraged.

"Okay, so, Luke, my name is Hayne, and I'm your brother's boyfriend. We've been together since last winter, so it's been a while now. I'm a painter, not houses you know, pictures. I did one of you, and I'm going to give it to your mom and dad. It's expressive, so they might not know what the painting means, but it's you."

Tears choked my throat. I'd seen him painting yesterday, with a permanent frown on his face. I wasn't allowed to look, and he tutted and fussed until it was dry and to his liking. He'd brought it with him, wrapped in paper, and left it propped up next to a tree by Mom and Dad's car.

"I love your brother, Luke, and I'll try to look after him as much as an emotional artist who gets lost in his work can." He huffed a soft laugh. "And I think Scott will look after me, too." He touched the marble again. "Happy birthday, Luke."

We stayed for a moment, quiet, and then Hayne eased away and left me alone for a while.

"Hayne's everything to me," I said. "You'd have liked him." I stared at my feet, forcing my hands into my pockets. "I'm sorry, Luke, sorry that you aren't here to meet him or see the things you should have seen. I've been lost without you, we all have, but I think Mom will be okay. She's more positive, focused, and Dad? He'll make it through the other side. I'm going to get him involved in the hockey kids I work with, and I think that will help."

I kissed the tips of my fingers and pressed the kiss to his name.

"Happy birthday, big brother. I'll be back to visit soon."

I walked back to Mom, Dad, and Hayne, just as Hayne passed them the painting. Mom carefully removed the paper and held up the canvas. It was smaller than Hayne usually worked on. Narrow and tall, and in splashes of red and gold, he'd copied the photo I had of Luke in my wallet. It was beautiful, lines that bled to the edge, and in the center, Luke was smiling.

"This will go in our new house," Mom's voice was choked with emotion. "Thank you."

Hayne smiled up at me, and the worry he'd had in his eyes this morning was gone. I held him close to my side, and a weight I didn't even know I'd been carrying lifted, my heart feeling lighter.

Maybe it was Luke telling me that everything was okay.

Who knows?

Hayne

"Oh, my stars and sugar knots, look at you!"

Mimi pinched my cheeks and kissed me on the chin, again, as a sharp wind tugged on my mortarboard. Scott plunked a hand down on my head, keeping my headgear in place. The stupid thing was too small. Well, I think it was that my hair was too curly, but whatever the issue, it refused to stay on. Mom had tried bobby pins, but they'd all fallen out by the time my name had been called and I had strolled up to get my degree in fine arts.

"My precious little artist, you've done such grand things with your life." Mimi kissed me once more, then moved on to Scott, smooching his cheeks as well, then adjusting his tie and patting down his lapels. "And this handsome young man is just one of those fine things!"

Scott's nose grew red. Mimi hooked his arm and dragged him to the other side of the restaurant. Mom giggled and dug into her purse, a tiny purple thing that matched her flowery plum-and-white summer dress. She looked so pretty all dressed up, so did Mimi. And Scott as well. All this fuss over me graduating. It felt weird and yet super nice.

"She's proud of you and Scott," Mom said, wetting a tissue, then scrubbing at the orange-red lipstick marks Mimi had left on my face. "I am too. And, honey." I glanced from Scott introducing Mimi to his parents, to Mom's pretty face. Her blue eyes were glistening with unshed tears. "Your father would be busting his buttons to see you here, a college graduate with a fine boyfriend and a new job."

"Mom, I'm the caretaker of the house Mr. Madsen bought. I'm literally living where I always have and doing the same things I always have, only now I'm getting paid to fix the bathroom sink when it drips."

She nodded and scrubbed at my chin harder. "I know, and there is nothing wrong with working while you create. Your grandmother did. I did. Hell, I still do. Poetry doesn't make the payments on the car, for the most part."

"I know. I'm proud of us too," I confessed.

She nodded and scrubbed with more authority on my

left cheek. "I think it's a fine way to start your young life. You have a job, a man who adores you, and a budding career in art. Yes, your father would be incredibly proud of you. He always said that you were going to be someone someday. And here you are. Being the man that he knew you would turn into, a caring, emotional, creative, loving man who's out and living life by his own rules and... and... and... oh shit."

The tears broke free, and she hurried to dab them up with her wet tissues.

I gathered her into my arms, my robes flowing around us, and hugged her tightly while she got herself together.

"He would have been so very proud." She kissed my cheek.

"Hey, you two okay over here?" Scott asked, sneaking up on us as best as a man his size could sneak.

"We're good," I told him, draping my arm over my mother's slim shoulders.

"Come here and let me kiss you too," Mom said, her eyes still dewy, as she reached for Scott's face, cupped it, and kissed him on both cheeks. So much kissing and shaking and backslapping today. I could barely keep my feet on the ground I was so elated with my life. "You take good care of him, understand?"

"Yes. Mrs. Ritter. I promise." Scott's laughing eyes darted to me. I rolled mine so hard my mortarboard tumbled off again.

"Make sure he eats and doesn't spend days in that attic doing nothing but painting. He does that, you know?" Mom said as she held Scott's head tightly between her hands.

"I promise I will make sure he eats and doesn't spend

all his time in the attic painting." His smile was bright and pure. I bent over to get my mortarboard, and when I stood, Mom had given him his freedom and was making her way to the table where both of our families were seated.

"You're the most beautiful man in the world, you know that?" He slid his fingers into my curls, fisted them, and then led my lips to his. Up on my toes I went, greedily needing the taste of him to get me through the rest of this wonderful, chaotic day. "It's going to be my sole goal in life all summer to make sure that all the time we spend in that attic isn't devoted to painting."

"What else is there to do in a hot, old attic all summer but paint?" I coyly asked, sliding my arms around his thick neck.

"I plan to show you."

He kissed me with promise. It was a vow made with passion and devotion and I knew for sure that our lives would be a kaleidoscope of brilliant, loving colors.

THE END

Coming next in the Owatonna U Hockey series

Benoit (Owatonna U, 3)

Benoit

When the lines between career and love blur, will Ethan and Ben find a way to create a future that will work for both of them?

Senior year is here, and everything is on the line. Benoit's time to shine in the crease is now, and he's going to do everything he can to make sure those professional scouts take notice. He's earned a great reputation for his skills in the net, and his laid-back demeanor is his key to maintaining his cool when things get heated in the goal crease . As the Eagles roar into a new season, Ben's laser-sharp focus is shattered by his attraction to Ethan Girard, the team's new defensive consultant. Trying his best to ignore the budding friendship that's taking a hard, fast turn into something far more passionate, Ben is determined to keep his mind on the sport he loves and not let his feelings for the handsome older man creep into his performance. But love, like hockey, is wildly unpredictable, and soon Ben finds that he's unable to distance himself from Ethan who is slowly and surely working himself into his heart.

Famed Boston defenseman, Ethan Girard, isn't stupid. Celebrating his thirty-second birthday in the emergency room after breaking his leg, and with a warning that healing will be a long process, he knows he has to think about his future. He was drafted at eighteen, and he's never known anything but hockey, but with no contract in place yet for the new season he considers that maybe it's time for him to hang up his skates for good. Volunteering to help out with the Owatonna Eagles fills his time, but from the moment he lays eyes on goalie Ben, he knows his world will never be the same again. Falling in lust is as easy as stealing his first kiss, but Ben refuses to engage. Has Ethan finally met his match?

Hockey Series' from RJ Scott & V.L. Locey

Harrisburg Railers

Owatonna U Hockey

Arizona Raptors

Boston Rebels

LA Storm

Chesterford Coyotes - Young Adult

Harrisburg Railers

When hockey wunderkind Tennant Rowe meets his new coach, he knows he's in trouble. Jared Madsen is nine years older than Tennant, impossibly attractive, and — worst of all — his brother's off-limits best friend. Is their chemistry worth the risk?

Changing Lines (Railers 1)

Can Tennant show Jared that age is just a number, and that love is all that matters?

The Rowe Brothers are famous hockey hotshots, but as the youngest of the trio, Tennant has always had to play against his brothers' reputations. To get out of their shadows, and against their advice, he accepts a trade to the Harrisburg Railers, where he runs into Jared Madsen. Mads is an old family friend and his brother's one-time teammate. Mads is Tennant's new coach. And Mads is the sexiest thing he's ever laid eyes on.

Jared Madsen's hockey career was cut short by a fault in his heart, but coaching keeps him close to the game. When Ten is traded to the team, his carefully organized world is thrown into chaos. Nine years his junior and his best friend's brother, he knows Ten is strictly off-limits, but as soon as he sees Ten's moves, on and off the ice, he knows that his heart could get him into trouble again.

Changing Lines

Harrisburg Railers (Hockey Romance)

Arizona Raptors

Coast to Coast (Arizona Raptors 1)

Coast To Coast

When opposites attract, this bottom-of-the-league team will never be the same again.

A stipulation in his father's will forces Mark back into the arms of a family that disowned him and leaves him one-third owner of a hockey team facing financial ruin. He doesn't even watch hockey, let alone like it, and wants nothing more than to head back to New York. Then there's the new coach, a stubborn, opinionated, irritating man with superiority issues and questionable music taste. Butting heads with Rowen becomes the new normal, but it comes with passionate debate and an all-consuming lust.

Challenged to rebuild one of the worst teams in the league into a future cup contender, Rowen can't pass up the opportunity. Never in his twenty years of hockey has he ever seen a team managed so badly or coached players overflowing with resentment and bigotry. Yet there's something about this team and this city that compels him to roll up his sleeves and start dismantling. If only Mark, one of three siblings who now own the Raptors, wasn't so damned rock-headed yet so damned appealing his job might be easier. It doesn't look like either is willing to give in, but one night in a dark, desert hotel changes everything.

Coast To Coast

Arizona Raptors (Hockey Romance)

1. Coast To Coast
2. Across the Pond
3. Shadow and Light
4. Sugar and Ice
5. School and Rock

Top Shelf (Boston Rebels 1)

Top Shelf

Acting on the attraction to his best friend's brother has always been off the table for Xander until a passionate hookup with Mason at a beach resort begins a love affair that burns long after summer ends.

Mason specializes in assisting same-sex couples on their journey to becoming parents and fighting every rule that blocks his way in the stuck-in-the-past agency that hired him. Living in his brother's pool house is rent-free, and every cent he earns he saves for his dream—that one day he'd have his own company helping others. The downside is that he has to see his annoying brother every day, the upside is that his brother's teammates from the Boston Rebels make regular visits. The eye candy that passes Mason's window is almost enough to make him consider dating a hockey player, but not just any player though. Ever since Xander —his brother's childhood friend—came out as gay at a press conference, Mason's puppy love has turned into a burning attraction he can no longer ignore.

Hockey has been one of Xander's main focuses since he was old enough to balance on skates. Well, hockey and Mason Kingsley, but Mason was always unattainable. Now that he's about to see thirty candles on his birthday cake and is no longer hiding the fact he's gay, he's ready to find a soul mate to make his life complete. A summer vacation is just what he needs to have time to think, but when the Boston Rebels arriving in paradise with Mason in tow, thinking is the last thing he needs. One torrid night under a balmy moon and rules about not messing with his best friend's brother vanish on a warm, tropical breeze.

Summer romances don't generally last past Labor Day, but with the new season about to begin Xander and Mason are going to have to face the world and decide if their love is real enough to withstand everything.

Top Shelf

Boston Rebels

Lost In Boston (Free Prequel Novella)

3. Snowed
4. Royal Lines
5. Blade
6. Rental

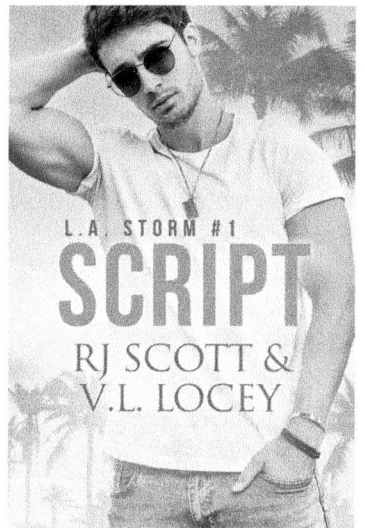

Script (LA Storm, 1)

Script

Hollywood A-lister Finn might be Canadian, but he needs Cameron to show him how to hockey.

Actor Finn Kerrigan is at a crossroads. After growing up a soap star, then starring in a hugely successful trilogy of action movies, he's finally given the chance to read a heartfelt and passionate script that could change his life forever. The role would be enough for people to see him as a serious actor, and maybe even win him an award or two (and no, a golden raspberry award for his action movies doesn't count). Once established as a serious actor he's sure he can come out of the closet and finally live his truth. When he lies to get the part of a hockey player on a struggling team, he suddenly has nowhere to hide. He might be Canadian, but the last time he skated he was ten, and no, he doesn't have hockey in his blood. With only a month until filming starts, he about to be exposed, but partnered with a player who's supposed to be giving him tips, he doesn't realize how many of his secrets will come to light. Falling in lust, one heated kiss at a time, is inevitable, but giving Cameron up at the end of the shoot could break his heart.

Cameron Chavkin is the face of the LA Storm. And the body, and the hair, and the smile. He's at the prime of his career, men and women want to be with him, and he's skating better than he ever has before. His house sits next to a famous rock star's mansion, his garage is filled with expensive cars, and he's even been asked to mentor a once-famous actor in a new hockey movie. Life is pretty sweet. Until the bad boy of hockey meets Finn, a man on the edge with more secrets than Cameron has endorsements. Knowing better than to get involved, Cameron is swept up despite himself, and when it's time to say goodbye to the Storm's most eligible bachelor is finding it hard to follow the script.

Script

LA Storm

1. Script
2. Second
3. Shield
4. Spiral

Off The Ice (Chesterford Coyotes, 1)

Off The Ice

A coming-of-age love story with high school, hockey rivalry, friendship, family, and coming out.

Soren's life changes in an instant when he and his younger brother are adopted by hockey royalty. Making sense of his new life is hard enough, but when he's enrolled in a private school it means facing a whole new set of problems. Navigating friendship, family, and hockey is one thing, but being attracted to the boy who vexes him is a whole new thing.

Felix has a reputation to protect. He's the kid who seems to have everything but looks can be deceiving. Spinning lies about his perfect life, he's created a fantasy world that even he has started to believe. Only, it's not long before everything crumbles, all of his pretty lies are revealed, and only his closest rival sees through his pain and stands by him.

Fighting is easy, friendship is hard, but love is everything.

Off The Ice

Chesterford Coyotes

Also By RJ Scott

For a full list of ebooks and links please scan the code above or
visit rjscott.co.uk/rjbooks

Meet RJ Scott

RJ discovered romance in books at a very young age and realized that if there wasn't romance on the page, she could create it in her head. With over one hundred and fifty books published, she is a full time author of gay romance.

She lives and works out of her home in the beautiful English countryside, spends her spare time reading, watching films, and enjoying time with her family.

The last time she had a week's break from writing she didn't like it one little bit and has yet to meet a box of chocolates she couldn't defeat.

www.rjscott.co.uk | rj@rjscott.co.uk

NEWSLETTER - rjscott.co.uk/rjnews

facebook.com/author.rjscott

x.com/Rjscott_author

instagram.com/rjscott_author

amazon.com/author/rj-scott

bookbub.com/authors/rj-scott

goodreads.com/rjscott

pinterest.com/rjscottauthor

Also By VL Locey

For a full list of ebooks and links please scan the code above or visit vllocey.com/stories-from-vl-locey

Meet V.L. Locey

V.L. Locey loves worn jeans, yoga, belly laughs, walking, reading and writing lusty tales, Greek mythology, the New York Rangers, comic books, and coffee.

(Not necessarily in that order.)

She shares her life with her husband, her daughter, one dog, two cats, a flock of assorted domestic fowl, and two Jersey steers.

When not writing spicy romances, she enjoys spending her day with her menagerie in the rolling hills of Pennsylvania with a cup of fresh java in hand.

vllocey.com
vicki@vllocey.com

Newsletter - vllocey.com/newsletter

facebook.com/V.L.Locey

x.com/vllocey

instagram.com/vl_locey

bookbub.com/authors/v-l-locey

goodreads.com/vllocey

pinterest.com/vllocey